The Woman He Couldn't Forget

Beth. He hadn't seen her in eight years—an eternity. And through those eight years, he'd been plagued with thoughts of what might have been, if he hadn't run out on her and Alana. Yet even while he'd been away, thousands of miles from Beth, he'd sometimes awakened from dreams so vivid he could still taste their forbidden kiss, the kiss that had changed everything...

For Jodie Ann Littlehorn, whose creativity and
friendship inspired this book, and for sisters everywhere,
whether united by the serendipity of birth or a
recognition of spirit.

**Vicki Lewis Thompson is also the author of these
novels in *Temptation*®**

MINGLED HEARTS
PROMISE ME SUNSHINE
AN IMPRACTICAL
  PASSION
THE FIX-IT MAN
AS TIME GOES BY
CUPID'S CAPER
THE FLIP SIDE
IMPULSE
BE MINE, VALENTINE
FOREVER MINE,
  VALENTINE
FULL COVERAGE
YOUR PLACE OR MINE
IT HAPPENED ONE
  WEEKEND
'TIS THE SEASON

ANYTHING GOES
ASK DR KATE
FOOLS RUSH IN
LOVERBOY
THE BOUNTY HUNTER
THE TRAILBLAZER
THE DRIFTER
THE LAWMAN
HOLDING OUT FOR A
  HERO
WEDDING SONG
MR VALENTINE

THE HEARTBREAKER

by

Vicki Lewis Thompson

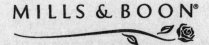

MILLS & BOON®

*MILLS & BOON and MILLS & BOON with the Rose Device
are registered trademarks of the publisher.
TEMPTATION is a registered trademark of
Harlequin Enterprises Limited, used under licence.*

*First published in Great Britain 1998
by Harlequin Mills & Boon Limited,
Eton House, 18-24 Paradise Road, Richmond, Surrey TW9 1SR*

© Vicki Lewis Thompson 1997

ISBN 0 263 81186 7

21-9807

*Printed and bound in Great Britain
by Caledonian International Book Manufacturing Ltd, Glasgow*

1

"WELL, PETE, I've sent my boy off to see your girl." Ernie Tremayne lay in the white hospital room alone and listened to the beep of the heart monitor punctuate the rumble of thunder outside. "Too bad I can't be there to referee, like in the old days."

A hell of a referee you were, Ernie, bribing those kids with ice cream if they'd stop arguing. Beth and Alana told me they used to start fights with Mike on purpose, just to get the damned ice cream!

Ernie chuckled, although it made his chest hurt where they'd opened him up. "Yeah, Mike told me that once, too. I miss those days, Pete. Miss 'em bad. This heart attack is a hellacious nuisance, but if it helps get those kids talkin' again, then it's okay."

A nurse walked by and poked her head in the door. "Mr. Tremayne? Visiting hours are...oh, you're alone."

"Yeah. Just talkin' to myself, Judy."

"Is there anything I can do for you? It's not quite time for your injection yet, but—"

"You got any cigars on you?"

She grinned. "Sorry. I smoked my last one an hour ago."

"There ain't nothin' you can do for me, then. You'd best go tend to some sick folks."

"Okay. Buzz the nurses' station if you need anything.

Besides cigars, that is." With a smile she backed out of the doorway and continued down the hall.

Ernie wondered what Judy would say if he told her he was talking to his old friend and business partner Pete Nightingale. Probably wasn't the first time she'd had patients in his particular fix, talking to dead friends and relatives. Of course she probably wouldn't believe that Pete answered back.

Ernie figured it was because he'd made contact with Pete during the few seconds he'd spent on the other side while the emergency room docs worked to get his heart beating again. Pete had been real glad to see him, and now they seemed to be able to talk to each other, which was a considerable comfort to Ernie, and he hoped it was the same for Pete.

Of course Ernie wouldn't mention any of this to the hospital staff. Sure as the world they'd write *Senile* on his chart, right next to *Heart Disease*. So Ernie kept the information strictly to himself. Someday, though, he might tell Beth and Alana.

THE EVENING DRIVE from Tucson Medical Center to the small town of Bisbee gave Mike Tremayne an hour and a half to consider what he'd say to Beth Nightingale when he saw her. He could start with an apology. Hell, he had a basketful of them to make.

What a mess he'd created eight years ago, alienating both sisters and ruining what had been the best friendships of his life. Worse than that, his guilt had kept him from spending time with his father. He'd only come home twice since he'd left town the night before he and Alana were to be married. His visits had been short, because like a damned coward, he'd been worried about running into Beth and Alana. For years he'd short-changed himself and the man he loved most in the world. Although Ernie hadn't spoken one word of reproach tonight in that sterile, frightening hospital room, Mike was filled with regret for the precious time he'd thrown away.

As he drove across the desert, storm clouds piled against the dark mountains and fragments of lightning cut through the blackness. The sweep of night sky and the sparse vegetation beneath it contrasted sharply with the jungle environment he'd become used to. But Arizona could be as wild in its way as the Amazon, and he'd always loved these dramatic summer storms. So had Alana, but Beth had cringed with every roll of thunder.

Beth. He hadn't seen her in eight years—an eternity. And through those eight years, he'd been plagued with thoughts of what might have been, if he hadn't run out on her and Alana. Yet even in the depths of the rain forest, thousands of miles away from Beth, he'd sometimes awakened from dreams so vivid he could still taste their forbidden kiss, the kiss that had changed everything....

THUNDER GROWLED in the distance as Beth opened the back door of her glass studio and hurried inside. Flipping on lights as she went, she passed through the workroom into the gift shop, where rainbow-hued examples of her art hung in the windows and from wrought-iron racks Ernie had made for her in his machine shop. Colby Huxford would arrive any minute. She wished she'd had time to eat dinner, but seeing Ernie at the hospital this afternoon had been more important.

Her visit to Ernie hadn't worked out as well as she'd hoped, though. She'd thought he'd be relieved that she'd found somebody to take over manufacturing the glass cutters they'd begun marketing under the Tremayne-Nightingale partnership agreement. Although she and Ernie would have to lease the patent to Handmade, Colby's Chicago-based company, at least orders would be filled on time.

But Ernie hadn't liked the idea at all. He'd begged her not to lease the patent, promising he'd be out of the hospital and back in his machine shop in a matter of days. She didn't believe that, much as she wanted to. Leasing the patent to Handmade seemed to be their only option.

As she surveyed the studio, her glance lingered on the large circle of stained glass that dominated the front display window. Inside the shop the colors lost their brilliance at night, but to anyone standing outside on the sidewalk, the interior lights made the piece glow with passionate intensity. She knew she was tempting Fate to leave it hanging there, but Ernie hadn't mentioned anything about Mike coming home, and the piece represented her finest work. Fortunately no one had guessed that it also represented the most sinfully glorious moment of her life.

Mike would guess immediately, but last she heard, he was headed off to guide another botany expedition into the Brazilian rain forest—living his dream. He'd been fascinated with the Amazon jungle ever since he was a kid. She still remembered the mural that had covered one wall of his room with a panorama of parrots, monkeys and jaguars roaming in a lush tropical setting. Mike had loved visits to the zoo and had vowed to see each of those same animals in the wild. But leading scientists into uncharted jungles meant he was often unreachable, and Ernie's doctors hadn't been able to contact him after the heart attack.

Still, it would be just like Mike to appear without notice. Perhaps she should take the stained-glass piece down, at least for the next few days. As she reached for the wooden frame to lift it from the hooks in the ceiling, a rental car pulled up to the curb in front of the studio. Beth abandoned the task as Colby Huxford got out of the car and started across the sidewalk.

JUST OUTSIDE of Bisbee Mike entered the tunnel that penetrated the Mule Mountains guarding the west entrance into town. Locals called it the Time Tunnel, and as Mike drove through it and looked down on the lights of the former mining town, he wished he really could go back in time, back to that night eight years ago. If he could wipe out the single stupidest thing he'd ever done in his life, everything would be different now.

The winding, mountainous streets of Bisbee were deserted at nine-thirty on a weeknight as Mike drove the rental car down Main toward Nightingale's Glass Studio. His father had told him it was called Nightingale's Daughter, now that Pete was dead, but the business partnership between the studio and Tremayne's Machine Shop remained intact. Anxiety constricted Mike's windpipe. He'd faced prowling jaguars and deadly vipers with more composure than this meeting with Beth. He would love to postpone it, but he'd promised his father he would talk to her tonight, before she made some irrevocable decision.

Apparently a business shark from Chicago wanted to take over the manufacture of the glass cutters that were Beth and Ernie's latest business venture. Ernie had asked Mike to step in and keep Beth from agreeing to anything. Mike had warned his father that Beth might throw him right back out again.

"Don't let her do that," Ernie had said. "The cutter

could make us lots of money. I think this Huxford fellow plans to swindle us out of it."

Some white knight he was, Mike thought as he neared the studio. Black sheep was more like it. But he'd try, for his father's sake, and for Beth's sake, too. He certainly owed her that much.

The studio, a brick two-story with a storefront below and living quarters above, sat in a row of nineteenth-century buildings along Main Street. Mike parked behind a nondescript sedan, no doubt Colby Huxford's rental. Ernie had said Beth would be meeting Huxford tonight, which was why Ernie had shooed Mike out of the hospital room and told him to get his behind back to Bisbee before it was too late.

Mike thought it might be eight years too late, but he got out of the car anyway and walked between the two vehicles to reach the curb. On his way he took his first good look at a large circle of stained glass hanging in the window. What he saw stopped him cold.

He stared at the work, a good thirty inches in diameter, and couldn't believe the scene created within it. Eight years disappeared in an instant, and his heart began to pound as memories came rushing back...her red silk dress whispering as he pulled her against him, her auburn hair caressing the back of his hand as she tilted her face up to his, her lily-of-the-valley fragrance surrounding him as he leaned close, inhaling her champagne-sweetened breath, touching his lips to hers...

And now they were captured in a circle of glass hanging in the studio window, frozen in their forbidden embrace.

Mike closed his eyes. He'd been slightly drunk and in a crazy mood. And that dress... Beth had never worn anything like it. He'd stupidly thought he could kiss her once, just to satisfy his curiosity before he became a married man. After all, he'd known her almost all his life, so what was the harm? But he'd known nothing—until his lips found hers. He could still feel the emotions that ran through him at that moment, the wonder of everything falling into place and the terror of knowing that everything would soon fall apart.

He'd tried to imagine telling Alana that he couldn't marry her because he was in love, and had probably always been in love, with her little sister. He simply couldn't imagine it. Alana had been a substitute mother for Beth ever since their real mother had died when they were five and three. He, of all people, understood the bond between the sisters, and everything in him rebelled at the thought of driving a wedge into that relationship. The simplest solution had been to leave town. Then they could both hate him, which he was pretty sure they did.

At least he had been sure until now, standing here looking at Beth's interpretation of that passionate kiss. For one hopeful moment, he imagined she'd put the work in the window as a signal to him. But that couldn't be. The doctors had spent a week trying to reach him and had caught him just as his float plane was about to leave Manaus. Another twenty-four hours and he'd have been deep in the rain forest, out of touch. Even Ernie hadn't known he was coming until he'd walked into the hospital room tonight.

He looked past the stained-glass piece into the studio and saw her standing inside, talking to a skinny guy in a gray suit. Nobody wore suits in Bisbee, so it had to be Huxford. Beth was listening intently, although she'd wrapped her arms around herself in a protective gesture.

His gut twisted at how beautiful she was. He'd forgotten, or else pushed her so far to the back of his mind it seemed like forgetting. He ran a hand over his day-old beard and wished he could have taken the time to shave and change out of his rumpled khaki shirt and chinos, but his dad had told him to hurry.

Now that he was here, hurrying didn't seem as important. He took some time to study her. She wore a long-sleeved purple blouse tucked into a flowing, ankle-length skirt patterned in purple and blue. The blouse clung to her breasts, and the skirt's waistband emphasized a figure as slim as he remembered when he'd held her in his arms. Beaded earrings dangled almost to her shoulders. He reacquainted himself with the delicate features and smooth skin that appeared as translucent as the glass she used in her work. She'd kept her hair the same luxurious length, and it rippled down to the middle of her back. The red highlights caught the gleam of the overhead fixtures as she moved behind the sales counter.

When Mike realized she'd gone after a pen, he swung into action. His appearance would do no good three seconds after she'd signed away the rights to the glass cutter.

The door to the studio was locked. He rapped on the glass set into the top panel of the door.

She glanced up, frowning. Then her eyes slowly widened, and her throat moved in a convulsive swallow. She put down the pen and came from behind the counter as if she were a sleepwalker. Huxford must have asked her something, because she turned her head briefly and spoke to him. Then she brought her attention right back to Mike.

Through the barrier of the glass in the door, he held

her gaze. This was no time to look away. As she drew closer, his heart slammed against his ribs. He'd gazed into the eyes of several lovers in eight years and had never had a reaction like this. He'd forgotten the mesmerizing intensity of those blue eyes. Yet her eyes didn't sparkle in welcome as they had so long ago. Instead they burned with a cold, deadly fire.

She twisted the lock and opened the door. "So, you're here."

"I came from TMC."

"I was just there this afternoon." She sounded out of breath. "Ernie didn't say anything about you coming home."

Mike allowed himself a smile. "He didn't know. Hello, Beth. It's great to see you again, too. You're looking terrific, as always."

Not even a glimmer of a smile answered his lame attempt at a joke. "What do you want?"

"World peace." When she moved to close the door, he added, "and a few moments of your time."

"I'm busy."

He massaged the back of his neck and sighed. How he longed to walk away. Although her icy response was exactly what he'd expected, it was still ripping him to shreds inside. But he remembered two things—his promise to his father, who was, after all, a partner in this business, and her circle of glass hanging in the front window. He lowered his voice. "Dad told me about Huxford and his offer. You're not going to sign anything tonight, are you?"

"That is none of your business. Good night, Michael."

He put out a hand to stop her from slamming the door in his face. "My dad's your business partner, correct?"

"That's correct."

"I'm his chosen representative, which makes this very much my business."

"Ernie sent you, then?"

"Yes. With a proposal. You owe it to him to listen."

Her shoulders slumped and she glanced away. "He shouldn't be concerned about what happens with the cutter." When she glanced up, the hardness was gone and anxiety shone from her eyes. "The doctors have warned him about stressing his system with unnecessary worry. He's supposed to stay calm and get better. Mike, he nearly—"

"I know." The words made it past the tightness in his throat.

"I blame myself." The words brimmed with misery. "We got a rush of orders, and I think maybe the pressure of getting them out brought this on."

"Don't you dare do that." His voice shook a little as the reality of his father's illness, a reality he'd been unwilling to face, set in at last. "He's been smoking those damned cigars since he was fifteen. And we won't even talk about his diet, all the ice cream, cheeseburgers, fries and shakes. This latest business venture didn't give him a heart attack, Beth. Don't even think it." He watched her struggle. She obviously needed the comfort of his words but was afraid to let down her guard. His heart ached for her, for him, for all of them. "Look, I know you don't want to deal with me, but Dad asked me to come here tonight and talk about an alternate plan. I promised him I would."

She hesitated a moment longer. "Okay, come in." She stepped back from the door. "Colby and I were just finishing up our discussion."

"Beth, you're not going to—"

"Not tonight. Besides, nothing can be done without

your dad's signature, anyway. I was just planning to give Colby a few references, people who've had success using the cutter.''

"Oh.'' He could have taken time for a shave, after all, he thought as he followed her into the studio.

BETH FOUGHT to stay composed as she introduced Mike to Colby Huxford. It was like introducing Indiana Jones to James Bond. The two were worlds apart in style and temperament. Beth could tell from the measured way they shook hands while keeping their expressions completely blank that they disliked each other on sight.

"Mike is Ernie Tremayne's son,'' Beth said. "He guides scientific expeditions in the Brazilian rain forest.''

"Ah.'' Colby pushed back the lapels of his suit jacket and propped his hands on his hips. "That explains the tiger's tooth, or whatever it is, around your neck.''

"Jaguar.''

"Whatever. Never felt the urge to go down there, myself. I hate snakes.''

"Really?'' Mike said. "They always speak well of you.''

"Mike.'' Beth sent him a warning glance.

"Never mind,'' Colby said. "I'd be edgy, too, if I'd just left my father's hospital room. Damn shame about that, Tremayne.''

"Yes, it is.''

"Could be the best thing for this glass cutter, though. Handmade can do a much better job of realizing its potential than a small operation could ever dream of doing.''

"Apparently you don't know Beth and my father very well,'' Mike said.

"We were doing fine until Ernie's attack,'' Beth

added. She realized she didn't like Colby any better than
Mike did, but she couldn't afford to have the reputation
of the Nightingale cutter tarnished so early in this new
venture. "It's getting late," she said to Colby, "and you
still have a long drive back to Tucson. Let me give you
those references so you can be on your way."

"I'm in no hurry," Colby said, glancing at Mike.

"Then I'll take the blame for ending the meeting."
Beth forced a smile. "I'm a little tired. I've had a long
day." She walked behind the counter and picked up the
pen she'd dropped when she'd looked up to see Mike
standing at the door. The pen shook in her fingers and
she gripped it more tightly to write out the names and
phone numbers of the customers who had agreed to
serve as references for the cutter.

She noticed Mike wandering over to look at *The Embrace* hanging in the window, and she clenched her jaw.
Of course he knew what it was. She'd just have to brazen
it out.

That wasn't going to be easy, considering how she
was reacting to his sudden arrival. Time was supposed
to dull emotions, but one look into the knowing depths
of those brown eyes and she was battling the same feelings of longing she'd fought most of her life. He would
have to show up right now—unshaven, tousled and sex-
ier than ever. She wondered if he'd killed the jaguar
whose tooth hung on a leather thong around his neck.
He seemed to bring the primitive lure of the jungle with
him into the shop, but then, life had always been more
exciting when Mike Tremayne was around. Despite his
rotten character, she would always love him, which was
something neither he nor Alana would ever find out.

Mike made no effort to create small talk with Colby,
and that was fine with her. Instead he continued to wan-

der around the studio examining her work. He'd been a fair stained-glass hobbyist as a kid, Beth remembered. Her father had helped them each make sun-catchers as Christmas presents one year, and Mike had turned out to be pretty adept at the process. Once he'd become a teenager, though, he'd abandoned the hobby as being too sissy. Alana had given it up, too, leaving only Beth, who'd become her father's apprentice. At times she'd envied Alana and Mike their freedom, but she'd cherished the special relationship she had with her father and Ernie, too.

She ripped the top page off the notepad, came back around the counter and handed it to Colby.

"I don't really need these, you know," he said. "I'm convinced the cutter is good."

"But you still don't know how good. Having you talk to our customers will let you know that. I don't want to discuss the cost of leasing the patent until you've checked with these people."

"All right. I'll call your references. But you're the one who told me the cutter has to get back in production immediately."

Her smile was grim. "I think we can wait another twenty-four hours."

"Then you'll be ready to sign the papers if I come back tomorrow night?"

"I still have to convince Ernie that this is the best course of action, but assuming I do, yes, we can probably finalize everything tomorrow night."

"I'm sure you'll convince Ernie."

"We'll see." She'd love to have another option, but she couldn't afford the going rate any other machine shop would charge her for the work.

Colby held out his hand. "Shall we say seven tomor-

row night? We can celebrate with dinner, if there's anywhere in Bisbee that has acceptable food."

Beth made the handshake brief. She *really* didn't like
this guy. "We have some of the best restaurants in
Southern Arizona," she said.

"Is that right? I never would have guessed. Well, see
you tomorrow night, then." He started toward the door.
"Good meeting you, Tremayne."

Mike waved an acknowledgment as Colby headed
out the door. Then he turned toward Beth. "What rock
did you find him under?"

"He works for a Chicago outfit called Handmade
that's trying to establish itself in the hobby market.
When Ernie and I first started selling the cutters, they
saw our video on the home shopping channel and con-
tacted us. At the time, we weren't interested in their offer to lease the patent and take over the manufacturing.
But now—"

"Now it would be even more stupid. Dad says you
have a winner."

"We need another six months, Mike." She glanced
outside as Colby's rental car pulled away from the curb.
Now she was totally alone with the man who had betrayed both her and her sister in a single evening. "I
can't wait for Ernie to recover and start making the cutters again. Our credibility will be destroyed if orders
show up late. Besides, even if we could wait, I don't
think Ernie should continue working at this pace, considering his bad heart."

"Neither do I." Mike put down the stained-glass
night-light he'd been inspecting. "Fortunately, you have
me."

"*You?*"

His tone was mild. "You sound as if it's a joke." He meandered over toward *The Embrace.*

"It is a joke." She suspected he'd deliberately moved closer to the incriminating circle of stained glass to taunt her. Any minute now he'd ask her about it. "You're not a machinist," she said.

"Sure I am." He ran a finger along the ebony wood frame of the piece. "I spent five summers working for Dad, and I even found work as a machinist in Brazil, between expeditions, when I needed the extra cash." He turned to her. "I'm qualified to produce the cutters for you, Beth."

Making a deal with Colby would be risking her financial future. She knew that going in. But making a deal with this man would be suicide for her emotional well-being. "And how long could you spare, Mike? Three days? That won't be much help."

He gave her a mock bow. "I'll stay as long as you need me, my lady."

That almost undid her, but she clenched her hands and forced herself not to react. "Six months?"

He flinched but didn't look away. "Sure, if it takes that long."

"Sorry, but I won't let you martyr yourself on my account. And don't kid yourself. You'd never last six months. We don't have piranhas in the streams around Bisbee, or ferocious jaguars, or man-eating crocodiles. You'd go crazy living so far from your precious rain forest, and we both know it."

A muscle worked in his jaw. "You're making this seem tougher than it has to be. Dad was planning to train a couple of people to help manufacture the cutters, anyway. I could train them, and once Dad comes home, he could supervise. I'd be out of here in six weeks, not six months."

She began to panic. He and Ernie had thought this plan out very thoroughly, and it might even work, except for the fact that having Mike around would be hell on earth for her. She took refuge in the truth. "I don't want you to stay, Mike."

Anger flared in his eyes. "Dammit, Beth, grow up. What happened eight years ago is no reason to jeopardize your future now."

She wanted to hit him. Instead she turned away and folded her arms. "It has nothing to do with maturity. I'm looking at this from a purely practical standpoint. Working with glass, which is how I earn my living, requires a calm mind. If I'm in a bad mood, I can't cut the glass without breaking it, so I've eliminated the negative influences in my life. I can't risk having you around."

He was silent for several seconds. "If I'm such a negative influence in your life," he said quietly, "then why am I hanging in your studio window?"

2

MIKE COULD TELL from the way Beth's shoulders tensed that she'd been dreading the question. But she had to know he'd ask about the stained-glass piece.

She kept her back to him. "I think you'd better leave."

"Sorry. You're not getting off that easy. I have a right to know why you made this."

"I don't have to explain anything."

She had a point. "Okay, supposing I want to buy it? I couldn't find a price tag. How much are you charging for..." He paused and consulted the small white card in a holder on the windowsill beneath the circle of colored glass. "For *The Embrace?*"

She muttered something he couldn't understand.

"I can't hear you." He stepped closer to her. "How much?"

She whirled to face him, her gaze stormy. "I said it's not for sale."

He considered that for a while and became more intrigued by the minute. "When did you make it?"

"What does it matter?"

"I guess it doesn't. The fact that you made it at all is what matters. You seem to hate me with a passion. Why would you deliberately create something that reminds you of a guy you hate?"

She shrugged, although her expression was anything

but nonchalant. "I'm an artist. What you see there is an abstract concept of two people who—"

"The hell it is! That's us, Beth."

Her skin flushed the delicate pink of his favorite rain forest orchid, but her gaze remained challenging. "So what?"

He gazed down at her belligerent expression, so at odds with the beauty and serenity of the piece they were discussing. "What does it mean?"

"Absolutely nothing."

He wanted to break through that angry mask and get at the truth. He had a feeling it would be very important to him. "I don't believe you."

"I don't care if you do or not."

"Ah, but I think you do care."

"That's your problem, then. You're a closed chapter in my life."

He waved an arm back toward the stained glass. "Which is why you have this hanging in the window and won't sell it?"

"The colors are nice, and people have become used to seeing it there."

"Dammit, Beth." Grief over his father and lack of sleep had rubbed his nerves raw. "Don't play games with me. I remember how you always got emotionally involved with the stuff you made. You wouldn't have created that piece if you didn't care about me."

"Wrong. It was an exercise, an experiment."

"An experiment, huh? Then let's try another one." He pulled her into his arms and took firm possession of her mouth.

For one joyous moment she responded, and all the pieces of his world fit together for that brief second of soft lips, warm breath and the sweet, remembered taste of Beth. Then she bit him.

With an oath he released her and put a hand to his mouth. When he took his fingers away, there was blood on them. He glanced at her while he reached in a back pocket for his bandanna.

She'd backed several feet away, and she was breathing as hard as he was. "Don't you *ever* try that again," she said.

He dabbed at his lip. "I'd have to give myself time to heal up first, that's for sure. Good thing the shaman sent me home with some medicinal herbs."

"If I'm supposed to be impressed because you know a shaman, I'm not."

"And here I was hoping you would be."

She glared at him through narrowed eyes. "You probably think your exotic travels make you so appealing you can waltz in here and pick up where you left off with whichever sister is handy. After all, we are completely interchangeable, you know."

He'd had about enough. "All right! I shouldn't have kissed you that night before the wedding. It was a *mistake*, one I've paid dearly for. I left town so I wouldn't cause problems between you two. Don't I get any credit for that?"

"You want me to believe that was some sort of noble gesture? You left town because you've always intended to see the Amazon. Besides that, your ego was wounded because Alana wouldn't go to bed with you the night before your wedding!"

"*What?*"

"You didn't think she'd tell me, did you? Well, she did, once she found out you'd left her standing at the altar without so much as a goodbye note. She said you'd begged her to make love to you, but she wanted to wait, and so that explained why you left in such a huff. I didn't have the heart to tell her that a couple of hours before, you'd dragged me off into a dark corner to kiss me. If Ernie hadn't come looking for us, you probably would have tried to seduce me, too!"

Mike stared at her in disbelief. "Beth, I didn't—"

"You broke my sister's heart." *And mine.* "I can't forgive you for that, Mike."

So Alana had lied about what had happened that night, he thought in despair. She'd probably sensed something was terribly wrong. She'd been the one who had wanted to make love, perhaps in a last-ditch attempt to bind him to her. With his freshly discovered yet unspoken feelings for Beth, he'd refused. But, he couldn't say that now and accuse Beth's beloved older sister of lying. Beth wouldn't believe him, and besides, her final accusation was correct: He had broken Alana's heart. "I didn't ask Ernie this, but does—does Alana still live in Bisbee?"

"None of your business."

He realized he'd never accomplish what his father wanted unless he got past her anger. He swallowed his pride. "Look, the three of us spent most of our childhood together. We had a secret hideout, and a special password, and spent our time doing crazy, stupid stuff like having water balloon fights and bubblegum-blowing contests. All those memories have to count for something."

She gazed at him. "What was the password?"

"Excuse me?"

"You just said we had a password for our secret hideout. If all those memories mean as much to you as you claim they do, you should remember the password."

"Do you remember it?"

"I asked you first."

"Damn."

"Nope, that wasn't it." A faint smile touched her mouth. Then it was gone.

He closed his eyes and thought hard. "It was a flower. I didn't want a flower but you two outvoted me, so I was stuck with this candy-ass flower as a password when I wanted *boa constrictor*." He opened his eyes. "I remembered boa constrictor. Does that count?"

"No, because it wasn't the one we voted to use." The smile stayed a little longer this time.

Then he looked into her blue eyes and remembered the password. "Periwinkle."

"Lucky guess."

Thunder echoed in a nearby canyon. The storm he'd outrun was catching up to him. "Does the password still work?" His lip seemed to have stopped bleeding so he tucked the bandanna into his hip pocket.

"What do you mean?"

"Does it still get me in?"

She gave him a quizzical look. "We don't have a secret hideout anymore, Mike."

"Oh, I think you do. You and Alana. And I haven't been allowed in for eight years."

Her expression took on the contemplative look he remembered from when they were kids. Beth had always been the thinker, the cautious one, while he and Alana had been the reckless adventurers. That was another reason he didn't think she'd just accidentally made the stained-glass version of their fateful kiss. While he'd been hacking through the jungle trying to forget that moment, she'd been haunted by it so much she'd had to re-create it in her art.

"Let me help you through this crisis with the glass cutter, Beth," he said. "For the sake of the good times."

"I don't think it would work." She glanced outside as a flash of lightning lit the deserted street.

He'd started on this campaign to grant Ernie's request and give him a better chance to recuperate. But after seeing Beth's stained-glass creation, his motivation had expanded. He wasn't sure how they'd ever work around the obstacle of Alana, but maybe, after all these years, it was time to try. "I think it could work."

She sighed. "No, Mike. Trust me on this one. It's not a good idea."

Years ago he'd been pretty good at guessing what Beth was thinking. It was a good guess that right now she was thinking about Alana. He decided to make an end run around the objection. "You never told me what Alana was doing these days."

Her glance was sharp, and at first it looked as if she might not answer at all. Finally she spoke. "She's formed her own company—Vacation Adventures, Inc. She takes families on action trips like rafting, rock climbing, canoeing, things like that. So far she hasn't done anything outside the country, but she has plans to expand to South America."

He understood Beth's accusatory tone. He and Alana had planned to go to South America together after they were married. "I'll bet she's good at taking families on trips," he said. "She's always been a people person." The storm moved closer.

"She's good at it." She met his gaze. "You and Alana always wanted an adventurous kind of life, and it looks as if you both got it."

"Where's she based?" He knew his interest would be

suspect. Beth would think he wanted to rekindle the flame with Alana, but that couldn't be helped right now.

"Phoenix. But if you were planning to see her, she's not there. A family hired her to take them canoeing in the Ozarks for two weeks. She left yesterday."

"I hadn't planned to go see her yet. I will eventually, because it's time I apologized for what I did. But right now I'm here to be with Dad and help you, if you'll let me."

Slowly she shook her head. "I appreciate Ernie coming up with the solution, but I think it would be best for everyone if he and I make a deal with Handmade. We'll lease them the patent, and—"

"And throw away Ernie's hope for a comfortable retirement."

She looked stricken. "Now wait a minute, Mike. There's no guarantee that this cutter will become that popular."

"He thinks it will. He gave me an entire infomercial on the Nightingale Glass Cutter. He said it makes cutting glass so easy everybody in the country will want to try it. He predicts it'll become as popular as home video cameras."

"Or it could be a total flop," she said. "Who knows?" Lightning flashed again, followed by a hard crack of thunder that would've gotten a reaction out of her in the old days. She didn't flinch.

"Dad's sure he knows, and it's driving him nuts, thinking that the two of you have a potential fortune in your grasp and you're about to throw it away because he's not here to help you. He thinks of himself as your protector, now that your dad's not around. He's sure that by having this heart attack, he's let you down. The only way to fix the problem is for me to take over in his place."

"When you lay a guilt trip on somebody, you don't mess around, do you?"

"Not if I think it will help my dad get better."

She frowned and looked away. "I wish we'd never decided to market the damn thing. At the time it seemed like a good idea for both of us, but I'm sorry we started it."

Mike glanced out the front window as fat raindrops splattered against it. "There's nothing we can do about that now." He returned his attention to Beth. "Look, he begged me to take over the operation for him and save you both from the clutches of this Huxford guy. If I report back that everything's taken care of, he'll be free to concentrate on getting better. If I tell him you've refused my offer, he'll lie in that hospital bed worrying about it. That's a guarantee."

She looked trapped, and he regretted that, but it couldn't be helped. Whatever their problems, he was determined they wouldn't interfere with his father's recovery. "So now what do you say?" he asked.

She fidgeted with a turquoise ring on her finger. "You know I'd do anything in the world for Ernie."

And not a damn thing for me, Mike thought sadly.

"But I can't afford to completely reject this offer from Handmade."

"Because you don't trust me to come through?"

She met his gaze. "Let's just say I don't trust the situation. I haven't seen you in eight years, Mike. I don't know you anymore."

As a hotheaded twenty-two-year-old he would have left the studio in disgust, but living among the primitive rain forest tribes had taught him many things, including patience. "Can you stall Huxford for a while?"

"I don't know."

The rain came down harder, drumming against the windows. "Why don't you see if you can buy two weeks? We'll know a lot in two weeks. If I'm a disappointment in any way, then you can take the Handmade offer."

"A two-week trial isn't going to satisfy Ernie, if what you say is true about his dedication to this project."

He noticed the phrase *if what you say is true* and gritted his teeth. Trust would be a scarce commodity for a while. Two weeks might not be long enough, but he'd have to make do. "If it's okay with you, we'll keep the two-week trial between us and just tell Ernie I'm taking over the operation. That way we'll buy him two weeks of healing time before anything more has to be discussed."

"I—"

Crack! The glare of lightning filled the studio, and then everything went black.

Instinctively he reached out. "Beth, don't be afr—"

"I'm not afraid." She pushed his hand away. "Stand right there while I get a candle. If you move around in the dark without knowing the place well, you might break something."

So thunder and lightning didn't frighten her anymore, he thought, standing perfectly still in the very dark room while he listened to the rain lash the outside of the building. Even the streetlights had been knocked out.

A glow emerged from the workroom in back, and Beth came out carrying a glass and tin lantern with a slender candle burning inside. Mike recognized the lantern, which Beth's father had bought across the border in

Mexico. As kids they hadn't been allowed to play with it, but whenever possible they'd smuggled it into their hideout anyway, so they could tell ghost stories by candlelight. He and Alana had told ghost stories, at any rate. Beth had cowered under an old quilt and listened, her eyes huge in her pale face.

She set the lantern on the counter and Mike walked over toward the circle of light. "You used to hate thunderstorms," he said.

She glanced at him. "I learned there were a lot worse things than storms."

"Yeah, there are." He was sure she was talking about Pete's death. Mike had been working in a machine shop in Manaus when Ernie had called to tell him Pete had died of a particularly fast-working strain of pneumonia. The two men had been friends and business partners for years, ever since they'd met in a group counseling session for widowers. Pete had been the artist and dreamer, while Ernie had balanced the relationship with a dose of practicality.

It had nearly killed Mike not to come home for the funeral, but after some agonizing he'd finally decided the best thing for everyone was for him to stay in Brazil and not chance opening old wounds at an already traumatic time.

Beth leaned an elbow against the counter and gazed at him across the circle of light. "Do you ever wish you could be six years old again, as free as a bird, with no idea that bad things can happen?"

"Sometimes. There's a tribe in the rain forest who lives like that. The forest provides everything for them, and they literally have no problems."

"I'm surprised you didn't just disappear into the forest with them."

"It wouldn't work. I already know too much about the so-called *civilized* world to be happy the way they are."

"Two weeks, huh?" she asked.

"Two weeks."

"Okay."

He let out a long breath. "Thanks. I know it will mean a lot to Dad."

"That's the only reason I'm doing it, Mike."

"I know." But he wasn't totally convinced. There was still the matter of the stained-glass version of their kiss. In his eight years of moving among people who spoke no English, he'd become good at picking up nonverbal cues. The stained-glass piece was the biggest one he'd ever seen.

"I hope I won't live to regret this," she added.

"At least I won't have to worry about regrets," he said.

"Oh? Why not?"

"If I screw this up, you'll probably kill me."

A gleam of resolve he remembered very well lit her eyes. "I will. Slowly, and with great relish."

He gazed down at her and thought about the first sweet taste of her lips a few moments ago, before she'd bitten him. And despite the sting in his lower lip, he wanted to kiss her again. He controlled the impulse. "Guess I'd better go up to the house and get some sleep. I'll make an early-morning run to Tucson to see Dad and tell him we're all set, but I should be back before noon. Maybe you can come by the shop during your lunch break and we'll go over the cutter design."

"All right." She hesitated. "Listen, maybe we should set some ground rules."

Apparently she realized he'd nearly kissed her again. "Whatever you say."

"You can think what you like about that piece I created, but it means nothing. Don't get any funny ideas."

He considered arguing with her and decided against it. "Understood. But I am curious about something. Has Alana seen *The Embrace?*"

"Yes."

"And what did she think of it?"

"She doesn't really pay much attention to my work. It's not her thing. She saw it and said something like *hey, that's different.* I told her it was a fantasy couple, and she never mentioned it again. She doesn't know what happened between us that night, and I've never told her."

Mike wasn't so sure that Alana was clueless, especially when he considered the pressure she'd put on him that night to make love. "I'm amazed she didn't figure out what she was looking at. That's the exact color of your hair, and you had on a red dress that night."

"She's probably forgotten about the red dress, and it would never occur to her that I'd have allowed you to kiss me. Besides, if I hadn't been drinking champagne at the rehearsal dinner, it wouldn't have happened."

So that was the lie she'd been telling herself, he thought. "Are you trying to say you were too smashed to think straight?"

"Well, not exactly, but my inhibitions were pretty much gone."

"You couldn't have been very drunk, Beth. You re-created every detail exactly, even that green-and-blue silk jacket I was so proud of."

"Artists remember those sort of things."

Or women in love? He couldn't—or wouldn't—accept her dismissal of the work's significance. Not yet, anyway. "If you say so." He pushed away from the counter. "Well, guess I'll take off."

"Let me light your way out." She picked up the lantern and started toward the door. "These wrought-iron stands can be tipped over if you're not careful as you walk by."

"Which is a diplomatic way of saying I'm like a bull in a china shop?"

"I don't remember you having a reputation for graceful movement."

"Maybe not, but you have to admit I've always been good with my hands."

She paused. "I thought we'd agreed on ground rules."

"What did I say?"

She glanced at him, her eyebrows lifted.

"You're hiring me to be a machinist," he protested. "Good hands are a plus for that kind of job."

"That's not what you meant by that statement and you know it. I don't intend to spend two weeks fending you off, Mike Tremayne."

"Don't worry. You won't be fending me off, Beth."

"Good. Incidentally, how did you come by that jaguar's tooth?"

"An old medicine man gave it to me. For good luck. See you tomorrow." He opened the door and stepped out into the rain. When he reached the driver's side of the car he looked back at the studio. She might have thought the downpour would conceal the fact that she was standing right where he'd left her. And he couldn't really see her, but the glow from the candle gave away her position.

He took courage from that small action, and from the belief that she'd let him kiss her on that night eight years ago because she'd wanted his kiss. And despite the painful mark of her teeth on his lower lip, he suspected that she still wanted it. Of course that didn't solve anything. The fact remained that he'd jilted her sister.

Eight years ago he'd been unwilling to put his needs and perhaps even Beth's needs ahead of that all-important relationship between the two sisters. But Alana and Beth had grown up, and each had her own business in separate towns. Things had changed. He just wasn't sure if they'd changed enough.

He switched on the ignition and turned on the car's headlights. Then, on a whim, he flashed them off and on again, knowing she was still watching him. He leaned down to see if she would respond with the lantern. The light was gone.

3

BETH STOOD IN THE DARK and watched the ruby taillights of Mike's car as it wound up the hill and out of sight. Hating herself for the impulse, she wanted to throw on her raincoat and follow him. The Tremayne house, a restored little Victorian, wasn't far up the hill, and after the way Mike had kissed her, she had no doubt of the reception she'd get if she appeared on his front porch. Just imagining it made her liquid with desire.

She hadn't been truthful with him in many ways. His exotic travels during the past eight years excited her more than she dared admit. She'd smothered her questions about the places he'd seen, the people he'd known, because having him describe his adventures would make her wish she'd shared them. How he and Alana would have laughed if she'd confessed her secret desire to explore the jungle with Mike, to experience that dark sensual land in the company of the man she loved. She didn't have Alana's willingness to challenge the wilderness alone, but with Mike by her side, she'd dare almost anything. Yet Mike had always planned to have those adventures with Alana, and Beth had remained silent when they teased her about her timid nature.

She'd tried to find a substitute for Mike, someone with whom she'd feel safe to go adventuring. But the biker she'd dated had been crude and unfeeling, and she'd broken off the affair quickly. Her relationship with the professional skydiver had lasted longer, but in the end he'd been too self-absorbed to create the kind of mutual respect she needed. She'd begun to resign herself to a life filled with the company of her artist friends and a satisfying career, but no grand passion for a man.

Now Mike had walked back into her life and within minutes, he'd created an ache so demanding that she trembled from the effort to conceal her need. She knew if he made love to her it would only be a fling, and still she wanted him. Only one thought kept her from throwing herself into his arms. Alana.

Beth was pretty sure Alana had never stopped loving Mike. Like Beth, she'd seemed to be searching for his double. Every man she brought home looked something like Mike, and a few even had the same first name. But she'd never committed herself to anyone for longer than a few months, and Beth thought that in the back of Alana's mind was the hope, nurtured for eight years, that Mike might come back and ask to be forgiven.

Well, he had come back, but Alana wasn't here. Beth was.

She longed to accept Handmade's offer and be done with the whole business, but if Ernie believed that much in the success of the cutter, she couldn't turn the patent over to Handmade without giving Mike's plan a trial. For all she knew the cutter might provide Ernie with a comfortable retirement, and she had no right to take that away from him unless she had no choice. As his business partner she had certain obligations, of course, but her concern went far beyond that. She cherished Ernie as if he were a second father. When he had the heart attack she'd panicked, knowing she wasn't strong enough to lose another loved one so soon after her father's death.

Alana hadn't been in much better shape. They'd clung

to each other in the hospital waiting room as if they were survivors of a shipwreck. When word came that Ernie would pull through, they'd screamed and danced around like maniacs. That had been less than a week ago, and Alana had considered canceling her canoeing trip so she could stay and keep tabs on Ernie. The doctors and Beth had convinced her to go, but she'd arranged to call tomorrow morning for an update on Ernie's condition. A wave of uneasiness washed over Beth at her next thought. She was seriously considering not telling Alana that Mike was home.

AS MIKE WALKED down the hospital corridor toward Ernie's room, he realized he'd make a bargain with the devil himself if it meant he'd have twenty more years to enjoy the company of his father. He'd spend more time in Bisbee, a lot more time. Hell, maybe he could take his father with him on a trip to the rain forest. He could easily picture Ernie with a crowd of natives sitting around a communal fire circle and sharing a gourd full of cassava beer. What a kick that would be.

But first his dad had to get stronger. As Mike neared the doorway to the room, he felt more prepared than he had been the night before to see his robust father reduced to an invalid. He was not prepared to find Ernie propped up against the pillows with a cigar clenched between his teeth.

"What the hell are you doing, committing suicide?" Mike cried, heading for the bed.

Ernie took the cigar from his mouth and grinned. "Fake."

Then Mike realized he didn't smell cigar smoke. But maybe Ernie was waiting for a private moment to light up. "Give it here, Dad."

His father dropped the stogie into Mike's outstretched hand. "Judy, one of the nurses, picked it up for me at a costume place. Brought it by this mornin', even though it's her day off. Mighty nice of her, I'd say."

"That depends on whether you can smoke this sucker. Knowing you, you could sweet-talk the nurses into bringing you a real one." Mike examined the cigar.

"Aw, it's just rubber, Mike. But I'm so used to having somethin' between my teeth that it feels good." He chuckled. "Really got you going, though, didn't I?"

Mike sighed with relief as he glanced at his father. "If this had been the real thing, I was ready to wring your neck and save the doctors all the trouble they're taking to keep you alive."

"Just what I figured. Now you're gonna become the gestapo, keeping track of everything I do."

"You've got that right." He handed the cigar back to Ernie and pulled up a chair. "And when I'm not around, Beth's going to take over."

"Now if that ain't gonna be a royal pain in the butt, having you two fuss over me."

"You asked for it, landing yourself in this mess. You'll get no sympathy from me, Dad. If necessary, I'll bring in my shaman friend from Brazil."

"Humph. Next thing I know, you'll want me wearing that there tooth of yours."

"Not a bad idea." Mike started to take off the leather thong.

"Nope. You keep it. I ain't wearing no tooth at my age." Ernie stuck the cigar in his mouth again. "How'd it go last night with Beth? You two hash things out okay?" His question sounded casual, but his glance was like a laser.

"Sure. Everything's fine."

Ernie made a grab for his cigar as it tumbled from his suddenly slack jaw. "Fine, did you say?"

"Sure. Why wouldn't it be?"

"For one thing, because you two haven't said so much as *howdy* to one another since that night you cut out."

Mike was determined to keep the conversation light. Ernie didn't need to worry about the depth of his problems with Beth and Alana. "People lose track of each other."

"This ain't been a case of losing track, and you know it. This has been more like noticing what track the other one's on—" he waved the cigar to the right "—and taking a track in the opposite direction." He swept the cigar to the left, then studied it. "Couldn't talk so good without my cigar, neither." He replaced the cigar between his teeth.

"Well, maybe we had a few problems connected with what happened, but that's all in the past. Everything's going to be fine, now."

"You got cold feet, is all. Didn't surprise me none. You weren't ready to get married. Like I've told you a hundred times, you should've explained that to Alana somewhere along the line. She wouldn't like it, but I'll bet the three of you could've patched things up. It's a crying shame, after all those years you kids played together, that you're not speakin' to one another."

Mike rolled his shoulders and stifled a yawn as he leaned back in the chair. "You're right, Dad. And I plan to talk things over with Alana, too. You'll see. The whole thing will be taken care of."

"That's good, Mike. Pete'll be glad to hear it."

Mike sat up straighter. "Did you say *will* be glad to hear it?" Ernie seemed totally alert, but maybe the drugs were affecting his mind, after all.

Ernie gave him a long look and chewed on his cigar. "Naw. You must've heard me wrong. I said Pete would've been glad to hear it."

"That's a relief. For a minute there I thought you'd started talking to ghosts."

"Not me. If I started doin' that they'd give me a rubber room instead of a rubber cigar." He shifted the fake stogie to the other corner of his mouth. "So Beth promised to give Huxford the boot?"

"Yep." It was close enough to the truth. Huxford would probably go back to Chicago if he couldn't expect any more action on the deal for another two weeks.

"And you're gonna make the cutters."

"Yep."

"Can you do it?"

Mike laughed. "This is a fine time to ask me that."

"Well, if you're the least bit shaky on it, I'll talk you through. If you remember anything of what I taught you, it'll be duck soup. You had good hands for it, as I recollect."

"Thanks. Exactly what I told Beth. And speaking of her, you can do something for me. Tell her I'm a good machinist the next time she comes in to see you, okay? She's not totally convinced I'm a fair hand with the equipment, even though I told her I picked up some jobs in Brazil, so I'm not even out of practice."

"She'll be okay once you start making them cutters. Beth's the kind you have to prove yourself to. Words don't do nothing for her."

"Yeah, I know. I remember the time I almost killed myself jumping the steps of the old brewery on my bike, just to prove to Beth I could do it."

Ernie nodded. "That took about eight stitches to fix.

And don't forget that idiotic skateboarding stunt down Tombstone Canyon Road, and the day you climbed the fence into the old mining pit. Showin' off for Beth was a regular stupidity of yours."

And so it had been, he realized now. He'd never risked his neck to impress Alana, which was strange considering she'd always claimed he was her boyfriend, and he'd always believed it was true. From the time they were six years old she'd appropriated him, and being a guy with other things on his mind like baseball and cars, he'd just followed the path of least resistance. Then somewhere around tenth grade he'd developed an honest-to-goodness crush on Alana, and that had settled things for good. They'd planned to get married, save their money and go to the jungles of South America together.

"What happened to your lip?"

Mike was jerked out of his reminiscent fog and had to scramble for an explanation. He could feel heat climbing up from his collar. "I, uh, hit it on the corner of the medicine cabinet door."

Ernie gazed at him and shifted his cigar to the other side of his mouth. "Is that so? Would that be the top corner or the bottom corner?"

"It—"

"I'm only askin' because if it was the bottom corner, you must've been bent over like a pretzel at the sink, and if it was the top corner, you must've been standin' on a box. Either way I'm having trouble picturing this accident."

"Maybe it would be best if we didn't discuss my lip, Dad."

"Looks like somebody bit you, Mike."

"I—"

"Time to draw some blood, Mr. Tremayne," said the nurse who bustled into the room.

Mike had never been so glad to see a member of the medical profession in his life. He pushed himself out of the chair. "I'd better get going. I'm supposed to meet Beth at noon at the shop."

Ernie grinned. "Want the nurse to take a look at that lip before you go?"

"Never mind." He glared at his father. "I want to get a good start on those cutters, so I won't be back in the morning, but I'll swing by tomorrow night."

"Beth said she'd come then, too. Why don't you drive up together and save the gas?"

"I don't know. She's pretty busy, so she might not be able to leave the same time I do."

"Her being too busy to drive up with you wouldn't have anything to do with the condition of your lip, would it?"

"Goodbye, Dad." He headed into the hallway followed by his father's dry chuckle.

ONCE THE NURSE was finished, Ernie settled in for a little doze. But first he had a report to make. "Well, Pete, I got good news and I got bad news."

If this is going to be that old joke about the buffalo chips, I don't want to hear it. That joke's got cobwebs a yard long.

"It's sort of a joke, but not about buffalo chips. Mike and Beth are talkin' to each other again. In fact, there's evidence they got a little chummier than just talkin'."

What kind of evidence?

"Unless I miss my guess, Mike kissed her. Then she bit him."

Beth? You must be talking about Alana. Beth hates violence.

"It wasn't Alana. She's on a trip right now. And Mike couldn't have rounded up some other woman to kiss that fast. Nope, Beth was the biter, Mike was the bitee."

Mike and Beth? Are you telling me that Theory C is correct, after all?

"That's where I'm putting my money."

Alana's not going to like this.

"I know, dammit. I hafta get out of this hospital bed so I can run interference."

But if you get out of the hospital bed, Mike will think he's not needed and take off for the Amazon again.

"You're right. But if somebody doesn't keep an eye on those kids, they'll screw things up again. We already have an injury."

If I know you, you'll think of something.

"I'll tell you this much, Pete. I'd think better if I had a real cigar instead of this damn rubber one."

BETH CLOSED UP the studio at ten minutes before noon. Business hadn't been very good so far that day, but then summers were traditionally slow, and she usually ended up in debt. Selling the cutters was designed to fix the seasonal slump problem, among others. If sales took off, her income wouldn't depend on her selling stained glass. She could eliminate the exhausting production of small sun-catchers that satisfied the tourist trade and concentrate on big installations that challenged her creativity.

She walked through a narrow side street to the public parking lot where she kept her truck. Ernie's shop was located in Warren, a small community adjacent to Bisbee, and it was too far to walk. As kids she, Mike and Alana had ridden there on their bikes many times, but Beth hadn't been on a bike in years.

A bike ride might have been more comfortable, she thought as she unlocked the truck. A hot morning after the night's downpour had left Bisbee steaming, and the cab was like an oven, even after she rolled down the windows and opened the vents. Although the truck's air conditioner had died the previous summer, she hadn't gotten it fixed because she was pumping all her spare money into the cutter project.

By the time she arrived at Tremayne's metal shop, she felt as if she'd just spent fifteen minutes in a sauna. Rummaging in the glove compartment, she found a scrunchy and enough hairpins to secure her damp, unruly hair on top of her head.

Mike had driven his dad's old truck to the shop, Beth noticed. She opened the front door and stepped into the air-conditioned interior with a sigh of relief. Mike wasn't out in the customer area. She called his name as she rounded the counter and headed into the rear of the building.

She found him sitting at his dad's bench, his back to her. Something about the set of his shoulders told her to go slow. "Mike, it's me."

He didn't turn around. "I've never been in this place when he wasn't here."

"Oh, Mike." Instinct overrode caution as she went to him and put her hands on his shoulders. He shuddered beneath her touch, and she knew his grief was very close to the surface. "I know," she murmured. "I'd never been in the studio without Dad being there, either. It's a shock, the first time."

"I've been such a fool, Beth. I thought he'd go on forever."

She massaged his shoulders gently. Touching him felt

so sinfully right. "He's made it through this crisis," she said. "He's got a lot of years left, Mike. He's tough."

"I know he's tough, but I've lost that fantasy that he'll always be there. This has forced me to face something I haven't wanted to think about. Someday he'll be gone...and he's all I've got."

"All? What about the time you've spent in Brazil? Surely you've made friends who are important to you."

"A few." He allowed his head to fall forward as he absorbed the massage. "I'm even an honorary member of a tribe."

"The ones that live like children, with no worries?"

"Yeah. They're terrific people, and I care what happens to them, but I don't really belong there. I'm still a vagabond in Brazil, a rolling stone that gathers no moss, and all that crap."

"Isn't that what you wanted?"

He sighed. "It's what I thought I wanted. But when I heard from Dad's doctor, when I really understood how close he came to dying, everything shifted. My whole perspective changed."

She continued to knead his shoulders. "Hey, don't go off the deep end. You always wanted a life of adventure. I hope you're not letting this throw you so much that you're considering a career as a machinist in Bisbee. That just wouldn't be you."

"I'm not so sure about that."

She felt a moment of panic. Mike was the keeper of the flame. As long as he sought adventure, then she could dream of one day doing the same. But if he gave up, what chance did she have? "This is an emotional time for you. Believe me, I know how it feels. You want to crawl into the nearest cave and surround yourself with all the things that make you feel safe. But eventually you start to heal, and safety isn't as important anymore. Don't tie yourself down to something that will become a straitjacket later, Mike."

"You're making a lot of sense. But then, you always did."

She decided a distraction might be just what he needed right now. She gave him a final squeeze and released her hold. "Ready to discuss the cutter design?"

"Sure." He stood and came over to the demonstration light table Ernie had set up. "I figured out this must be it."

"Your dad thought we should have a cutter set up and operational, so either one of us could demonstrate it."

"So demonstrate."

"Better than that, I'll let you use it. It'll probably help while you're working on the cutters, if you know exactly what they're supposed to do." She glanced around the tidy shop. "I think he kept some glass somewhere."

"Yeah, I saw it. Just a minute." Mike walked over to a cabinet and came back with a notebook-size piece of cobalt glass. "Will this do?"

"Perfect. We'll need some sort of pattern." She grabbed a sheet of paper and a pen and drew a heart. Instantly she regretted her choice of shapes, but Mike had already come up beside her, and making a big deal about the design would be worse than just using it. She positioned the heart outline on the light table, switched on the lamp underneath and put the blue glass over the drawing. Then she adjusted the jointed metal arm clamped to the table so the cutting wheel was over the glass.

"Go ahead and try it." She stepped back and motioned him toward the table. "You're going to be amazed at how easy a two-handed wheel makes the whole process."

"Okay, what do I do?"

"Grip the handles like this." After months of demonstrating the cutter, she automatically reached around him and covered his hands with hers. Belatedly she realized how cozy the position was, and how unsettling. "Now position the wheel where you want to start your cut," she continued, "and apply pressure as you guide it around the lines."

"How much pressure?"

She tried to keep her breasts from brushing his back but it was nearly impossible. She forced herself to concentrate on the cutter and pretend she was demonstrating it for a stranger—better yet, an elderly lady with false teeth and arch supports. "Listen for a scratching sound. That means you're scoring the glass. You've done this before. You'll know when it's working." His hands beneath hers weren't the hands of an elderly lady. Instead she felt strong tendons and the sensuous tickle of hair against her palms. The tangy scent of his aftershave filled her with images of snuggling against him and lifting her mouth for his kiss. This had been a very bad idea.

She gritted her teeth and watched the wheel bite into the cobalt glass. "That's it. Now, steer around the curve. Good. I'm letting go, now." She backed away with a barely audible sigh of relief and put a hand over her pounding heart. "Keep that same pressure as you finish the outline. There. Excellent."

He released the cutter handles and picked up the glass. It broke away cleanly on the score lines into a perfect heart shape. "Amazing. I can see what Dad's talking about. You could manage this with no training at all. Even kids could do it."

Gradually her pulse regained its normal rhythm. "My father came up with the idea after he struggled through teaching a class at a retirement home using the old-style cutter. But he...died before he and Ernie could market it." She still couldn't say that without a sharp stab of regret.

Mike turned to face her, his expression tender. "That's the other reason my dad wants this to be a success, isn't it? As a tribute to Pete."

"That's—" She paused to clear her throat. "That's one of the reasons I want it to be a success, too."

"He was a great guy," Mike said softly.

She couldn't stop the flood of pain. "Then why didn't you come home when he died, Mike? He was like a father to you!"

He flinched as if she'd slapped him. Then he took a deep breath. "Within an hour of the time I heard about your dad, I had an airline ticket in my hand. But then, while I was sitting at the gate I thought about it and finally figured you and Alana had enough to deal with, without having me around. I called Dad back, and he said he was holding up okay, so in the interests of keeping the peace, I tore up the ticket. If it's any consolation, I wish I hadn't. I shouldn't have left my father alone at a time like that, no matter what the consequences to you and Alana."

She was stunned. "You put aside your own grief because you thought we wouldn't want to see you?"

"My grief wasn't important. But I should have been here for my dad."

"How can you say your grief wasn't important?"

He shrugged. "I'm a guy. I'm supposed to be tough about those things, right?"

"And were you tough?"

He looked away. The jaguar tooth around his neck quivered as he swallowed a lump of emotion.

Pain squeezed her heart as she pictured him leaving the airline terminal and going back to some impersonal room where he'd undoubtedly wept alone for the man who'd helped raise him. "Oh, Mike." She slipped her arms around him and laid her cheek on his chest. "I'm so sorry," she murmured, holding him gently.

With a long sigh he wrapped her in his arms and rested his cheek on her hair. "I've missed you, Beth."

"I've missed you, too." Holding him was heaven, but no matter how much she wanted to comfort him, she dared not stay too long. Slowly she extricated herself, stepping away as she broached the one subject that might save her from doing the unthinkable. "Alana called this morning."

He regarded her intently. "Did you tell her I was here?"

Her courage flagged and she looked away from that piercing gaze. "Uh, no, I didn't."

"Why not?"

"She's...she's in the middle of an important trip. Her business is just getting off the ground, and if she left that family in the middle of their vacation, there'd be hell to pay."

"And you think she would leave them if she heard I was here?"

"I don't know. She might."

Mike captured her chin and forced her to look at him. "Is that the only reason you didn't tell her?"

Her pulse quickened. His knowing gaze saw far too much. "Mike, please."

His hand gentled and slid along her jawline. "You said you missed me. What was it about me that you missed?"

She should move away. Letting him touch her this way, considering how low her resistance was already, would have predictable results. Yet she seemed to have grown roots. "You...were like the brother I never had."

He reached up with his other hand and began taking the pins from her hair. "And that's how you think of me? Like a brother?"

"Of course."

"Were you treating me like a brother when you demonstrated the cutter just now? Was I the only one going crazy when you touched me?"

"I—" She swallowed as he freed her hair and tossed the scrunchy and hairpins onto the light table. "Mike, stop..."

He combed her hair with his fingers as he gazed deep into her eyes. "I don't think you'd tremble like this if a brother decided to take your hair down."

"I have to go." Yet she couldn't move.

"You can leave in a minute." He slipped one hand behind her head, cradling it. "Right after I kiss you."

Her heartbeat thundered in her ears. "Mike—"

"Two things," he said, hovering nearer. "One, don't bite me. Two, I am not your brother." Then his mouth settled over hers.

4

MIKE LONGED TO CRUSH Beth to him and bury his pain in an orgy of passion, but being exposed to the depth of his need might scare her away. And his needs were deeper than even he had realized. Her touch, her gentle voice and her empathy had created a thirst he could not deny. He couldn't let her leave without holding her once more and drinking sweet comfort from her lips.

At first he kept the pressure of his mouth light, the kiss almost platonic. Almost. Tasting her again made his head swim. Her scent was spicier and more womanly than it had been eight years ago, but her mouth was a re-membered wonder, her kiss the beginning of a journey he knew he must take one day or lose his sanity.

As the velvet firmness of her lips softened a fraction, he allowed himself the smallest aggression, subtly coax-ing her to open to him. Her lips parted slowly, cau-tiously. He fought the needs coursing through him and took only as much as she offered, then gently urged her to offer more.

Heart hammering, he drew the tip of her tongue into his mouth. She trembled, and he steadied her with a hand at her waist while he stroked his tongue against hers. Her soft moan told him she might allow more. He didn't take more.

Instead he lifted his head and opened his eyes. There. That was the moment he'd dreamed of, the moment he'd been denied twice—once when Ernie had called to them and brought an abrupt end to their kiss, and last night, when she bit him. Her eyes remained closed, her dark lashes resting against cheeks tinged pink with desire, her mouth rosy and ripe with promise. How he longed to return there. Yet he waited.

Her eyes drifted open, and all his dreams found an answer in their shadowy blue depths.

Then she squeezed her eyes shut and pushed away from him. "That was despicable of me."

"No. Beth—"

"I'm going to ask you to ignore what just happened." She straightened her shoulders and looked him square in the face, as if she were facing a firing squad. "Please."

"I can't." His voice was raw from wanting her.

"Suit yourself. I'm going to ignore it."

"I don't think you can, either." He could even prove the point by taking her in his arms again, but he wouldn't. Not if it made her hate herself. "There's something between us, Beth. I think there always has been."

She drew in a breath and took another step backward. "Okay, I won't deny that I...I'm attracted to you. But that doesn't mean I'll ever do anything about it."

"Why not?"

"I can't believe you have to ask."

"I'm not engaged to Alana anymore. I never plan to be engaged to her again. We're all different people, now."

"Are you different?" She pulled her hair back and grabbed the elasticized fabric from the worktable. The action caused her breasts to push against the thin material of her sleeveless shirt. "Or are you just acting true to form, going after the most available woman around?"

The words stung, and he lashed back. "Ah, so that's your other reason for shoving me away. You think I only kissed you because you're the female who happens to be here. If Cindy Crawford was around, I'd be kissing her, or if she couldn't make it and Demi Moore showed up, I'd try to seduce Demi. Is that the idea?"

"More or less." She secured her hair on top of her head with the hairpins, lifting her arms in a graceful motion as she finished the task.

Despite his anger, he ached to press his mouth against the creamy underside of her arm, to hold her hands above her head and kiss the hollow of her throat, the angle of her collarbone, the shadowed cleft between her breasts.

"You happen to like women, Mike," she continued. "And they like you, obviously. You're a man of the world, now, one who's probably experienced some... unusual sexual customs in your travels."

In reality he'd discovered more similarities than differences in sexual practices, but he decided to foster the image she held. "I suppose you picture me cavorting with bare-breasted native women."

"Well, have you?"

"I'm a man, Beth. I didn't live like a monk while I was in Brazil."

"And were your experiences...different?"

"Yes." He paused. "Does that excite you?" The question was unnecessary, he thought. Her quickened breathing and the fire in her eyes gave him the answer. "The women I made love to in the rain forest have a freedom about their behavior," he added. "They don't play games. Instead they're interested in satisfying a basic human need."

"Life isn't always that simple."

"Apparently not."

She took a deep breath. "Knowing that Alana still cares for you, I couldn't live with myself if you and I..."

"Then you must also feel guilty for not telling her I'm here."

"I do, but I don't want her to jeopardize her business."

His gaze was unrelenting. "Wouldn't that be her move, not yours?"

She hesitated, as if to argue, then nodded. "Yes. I should have told her."

"But you didn't. And my guess is that your hidden reason, way in the back of your mind, was that you and I could let this attraction take its natural course, and she'd never have to know."

She blushed. "God, you force me to be honest with myself! Yes, okay, I probably did think that, and I'm not proud of it. And now that you've stated it so baldly, I realize I could never give into that kind of sneaky behavior, so just forget it, Mike."

He gazed at her with amusement. "Highly unlikely that I can do that, Beth."

"Well, try!"

"Look, I would never want to hurt you or Alana any more than I already have, but I don't think we can just ignore whatever's between us. Alana's kiss hasn't haunted me for eight years. Yours has."

The light that ignited in her eyes was soon doused, as if by a conscious act of will. "That's pretty convenient, considering I'm the one in Bisbee and Alana's in the Ozarks."

He gave her a weary grin. "There you are again, old prove-it-to-me Beth. You really haven't changed, have you?"

"I've changed a lot."

"But you still want cold, hard evidence. Like when I

had to jump my bike off the brewery steps. I can still picture you putting your fists on those skinny little hips and saying, *Prove it, Mikey.* So damned if I didn't try to prove it to you."

"Oh, I'm sure that you did it for Alana, not me. I just happened to be along."

"Let me refresh your memory," he said. "Alana wasn't there. And the time I skateboarded down Tombstone Canyon Road and just about killed myself, Alana wasn't there. And when I climbed over the fence into the open-pit mine and almost fell four hundred feet, Alana wasn't there. I did those things to impress you, not Alana."

"But Alana was the one who—"

"Who told me I was her boyfriend. At that age you don't argue. You don't even know what's going on. You go with the flow. A teenage crush somehow escalates into wedding plans. And then, one champagne-filled night, you make a mistake, or maybe you finally follow your heart, and you're holding the other sister in your arms. Then—"

"I don't want to hear this." She put her hands over her ears in a gesture that came straight from their childhood. Her cheeks grew pink as she took them away again immediately and straightened in an apparent attempt to seem more adult. "I think you're rewriting history."

"Maybe. Or maybe eight years in the jungle gives a guy some perspective."

She ran a tongue nervously over her lips. "I need to get back to the studio."

He followed the direction of her tongue and a sweet ache invaded his groin. "And I need to settle in here and get used to the equipment so I can start turning out some cutters for you." He remembered that she had an appointment with Huxford tonight. "Want me to come over and hang around while you give our friend from Chicago the bad news?"

"No. Thanks for offering, but I'll handle it."

"He planned to buy you dinner, didn't he?"

"I don't think he will, under the circumstances."

"Then let me."

"Mike, that's really not a good idea. The less we see of each other socially, the better."

"Or maybe if we spend some time together we'll figure this thing out. Is Café Roca as good as it used to be?"

"Yes, but—"

"We can meet there if you don't want me to pick you up. Then we can each go home to our respective places."

"You're not driving into Tucson to see Ernie?"

"No. When I was there this morning I told him I'd be staying at the shop late to get ready for a full day of work tomorrow." He could tell she was tempted. "Come on, Beth. I don't have any buddies in town anymore, and I don't want to eat hot dogs and beans by myself tonight."

She smiled. "Is that what's in your father's cupboard?"

"Mostly. Ernie's not much on gourmet food, which is okay because I never learned to cook, either, except over a campfire."

She sighed. "Okay, we can have dinner. Dutch."

"Listen, I'd like to—"

"No, you listen. Dutch," she said. "Give me about forty-five minutes with Colby. I'll meet you at the restaurant about quarter to eight, if you'll be through at the shop by then."

"I'll be through." He gazed at her. "If I came by for

you, it might be easier to get rid of him in case he's still around."

"Mike, I'm a big girl. I'll handle Colby."

"Okay." He forced himself to accept that. He wanted like hell to go to the studio and make sure Huxford had been kicked out of town, but she didn't want him to, so he'd meet her at the restaurant. They'd share a meal and a bottle of wine. And then...they'd see.

COLBY ARRIVED at the studio while Beth was behind the counter totaling the day's receipts. His dark hair was slicked back as usual, and he wore what Beth concluded was casual dress for a guy like him—an open-necked shirt, slacks and a blazer. She hoped he was careful to stay in air-conditioned cars or buildings; otherwise he'd pass out with all those layers on. She suspected he liked the padded-shoulder effect of a suit or blazer, whereas some men, like Mike, for example, didn't need the help. Then she chastised herself for making the comparison. Mike's body was not a topic she cared to think about.

"Have a good day?" Colby asked, laying his briefcase on the studio's sales counter.

Beth's traitorous mind offered up a Technicolor, sensory-enhanced picture of Mike's kiss. "An eventful day," she said.

"Ready to sign the lease agreement and go out for a good meal?"

Beth folded her hands and placed them on the counter while she met Colby's gaze. His gray eyes, usually as businesslike as a flannel suit, were warm with approval as he surveyed her. That was the first moment she realized he was interested in more than a contract for her cutter. He probably thought everything was as good as settled, and his matter-of-fact approach had given way to frank appreciation.

She hadn't helped any by the way she was dressed, but she'd been thinking about having dinner with Mike when she'd put on the scoop-necked white gauze dress and the blue beaded earrings that matched her eyes. Not that she wanted to impress Mike, of course. But she didn't want to appear for dinner looking like a hag, either. She hadn't factored in the possibility that Colby would think she'd dressed for dinner with him, instead.

"I suppose you have a flight scheduled back to Chicago tomorrow," she said, supposing nothing of the kind.

He leaned against the counter in a show of easy familiarity. "Actually I thought I'd courier the contract back to Chicago and take a little vacation."

"Oh?" She didn't like this, didn't like it at all. "Where are you going?" As if he was going anywhere. She knew that look, and it meant a guy had plans, and dinner was only the first phase.

"I booked a room at one of your bed-and-breakfast places. Your remark about the good restaurants in Bisbee made me realize I'd barely taken time to see the area." He smiled, displaying his teeth. "I thought you might have some time to show me around."

For one weak moment she wished she'd taken Mike up on his offer to hang around while she delivered the news to Colby. She took a deep breath, reviewed why it was important to rely on herself instead of someone else, especially someone as unpredictable as Mike, and the moment passed.

"I don't think I'll have much time to show you around, Colby. I—"

"But the cutter will be off your mind, and I've noticed

that your studio doesn't do much business this time of year, so I thought maybe—"

"That's just it. The cutter won't be off my mind. I'd like a two-week extension before I finalize the leasing agreement."

The smile disappeared. *"Two weeks?* Why on earth would you want to wait two weeks? By that time your customers will be banging on your door and demanding their cutter."

"I've made arrangements to have someone manufacture it here in Bisbee."

His eyes narrowed. "Who?"

"Ernie Tremayne's son, Mike."

"The great white hunter type I met here last night?"

"Yes." Beth clenched her jaw but kept her tone polite. She didn't want to turn this man away forever. She might still need the deal he offered. "He's trained as a machinist and has offered to take over the manufacture until Ernie's on his feet."

"Beth, you're making a big mistake."

Probably, she thought. "No matter how generous Handmade's terms are, Ernie and I would still be better off with a hundred percent of the profits, Colby. Mike thinks we can patch together a manufacturing program that will work for me. I've decided not to sign away the rights until I give him a two-week trial."

Colby's facial muscles tightened. "You can't ask for an extension and expect the same deal you'd get if you leased us the patent now. In two weeks you'll be more desperate, and my company will expect me to capitalize on that. It's nothing personal, but that's how the business world operates."

"I know perfectly well how the business world operates."

"I don't think so. If you were more savvy, you'd put your bet on a sure thing instead of letting this Tremayne guy talk you into gambling on him. What is he, an old boyfriend or something?"

"No," she said quickly, then wished she hadn't even answered the question.

His eyebrows lifted.

"Even if he were, which I assure you he's not, that's not an appropriate thing for us to discuss."

"It is completely appropriate if your involvement with him is ruining the deal I've been working for three days to complete."

"I regret the time you think you've wasted, but as you've said, you'll probably get a lease on the patent anyway, and on terms more favorable to Handmade. Two weeks means a lot to me, but it can't be a significant time period for your company."

"You're right, it isn't. I was thinking of your welfare. You're not using your head."

She was heartily sick of the discussion. A surreptitious glance at her watch told her she needed to finish closing up the studio or she'd be late meeting Mike. "You're probably right. We'll see, won't we?"

"I suppose we will. I can't force you to sign the agreement."

"Considering the two-week delay, I imagine you'll want to catch a flight back to Chicago in the morning instead of hanging around Bisbee."

His gaze was calculating. "Trying to get rid of me, Beth?"

"Of course not," she lied. "But I won't be able to show you around, and it gets pretty hot here in August, as you've probably noticed."

"As it happens, Chicago's in the middle of a heat

wave. I know what that's like after living there for thirty-four years. I don't know what summer in Bisbee is like. People in Tucson say it's milder here at four thousand feet."

"Not that mild. And not everyone has air-conditioning, either."

"If I didn't know better, I'd say you're trying to discourage me from staying."

"Colby, if you want to spend your vacation here, it's fine with me." Fortunately he didn't know her well enough to accuse her of lying through her teeth. One look at her flushed cheeks, and Mike would have done exactly that.

"Then I think I will spend my vacation here, thank you. Now, shall we go have that dinner we talked about?"

"But...but we didn't finalize the deal."

He smiled again. "Now I would be some sort of louse if I backed out of dinner because you didn't put your name on the dotted line. Of course I'm still taking you to dinner."

"Well, Colby, this is a little awkward." She glanced down at the counter. "I knew I wouldn't be signing the lease agreement, and I thought under those circumstances you wouldn't want to have dinner, so I made other arrangements."

"So Tremayne not only snatched that lease agreement from under my nose, he stole my dinner partner, too."

She glanced up. "What makes you think that?"

"I saw the way he looked at you last night. I don't know what your history is with the guy, but I know what he'd like his immediate future to be when it comes to you. The cutter's just an excuse to put him in constant contact."

Beth lifted her chin. "Although this really isn't your business, as I said, Mike is doing this for his father, not for me."

"And who told you that?"

"Mike did."

"And you believed him?"

"Yes." But come to think of it, she hadn't spoken to Ernie to confirm that the plan was his idea. It was slightly possible that this whole scheme had been cooked up by Mike. Probably not, but there was that outside chance and she shouldn't be lulled into trusting Mike's word too quickly.

"I can see by the expression on that lovely face that I've started you thinking, at least." Colby picked up his briefcase from the counter. "I can take a rain check on that dinner. Tomorrow night?"

"I'll be driving into Tucson to see Ernie tomorrow night."

"I see." Colby's glance swept over her. "Well, I always did like a challenge. I'll drop by tomorrow to say hello."

"Fine."

Colby started toward the door. When his hand was on the knob, he turned back to her. "And when you see Ernie, I'd ask a few pointed questions, if I were you. This cutter is too important to your financial future to allow Mike Tremayne to use it as a pawn for his romantic conquests."

Beth chose not to answer him.

He left with a two-fingered salute in her direction.

As he drove away in his rental car Beth made a decision. Before dinner, she and Mike were going to use the phone at the art gallery next door to the restaurant and make a friendly call to Ernie's hospital room. Mike couldn't object to the two of them wishing his father a pleasant night. And in the process, she just might learn a few things. She didn't intend to wait twenty-four hours to find out whether Mike was still the double-dealing rogue he'd been eight years ago.

5

AFTER SETTING THE SECURITY system alarm, Beth left the studio by the front door and stepped out into the kind of summer night that always reminded her of Alana's wedding rehearsal dinner...and Mike. The temperature had dropped to about eighty degrees, and a slight breeze stirred the jasmine-scented air. Decorative lights strung across Main Street for a wine festival the previous weekend were still up, and some town official had decided to turn them on tonight, a typically spontaneous gesture in Bisbee.

She'd tried all afternoon to be nonchalant about her dinner with Mike, but she hadn't succeeded. Anticipation bubbled within her as she walked down the uneven sidewalk toward the restaurant. When she was a teenager madly in love with him, she'd often fantasized about nights like this. She remembered watching with envy from her bedroom window as Mike and Alana had left, arms around each other, to share a table at one of the local restaurants. Alone in her room, she'd mentally recreated the entire scene as she'd imagined it taking place—the softly lit romantic atmosphere, the hands clasped across the table, the fond looks, the good-night kiss.

Of course she'd pictured herself as Mike's date instead of Alana. Perhaps that's why she'd been unable to resist his invitation for tonight. Not that she would allow hands clasped across the table or fond looks, and the good-night kiss was definitely out, but she could sit with Mike for one special meal and live at least a portion of her teenage fantasy. Café Roca had some of the best romantic atmosphere in town.

First, however, she intended to make that call to Ernie, with Mike right by her side. If it turned out that Ernie knew nothing of Mike's plan to manufacture the cutters for her, then the evening might not be quite as peaceful as she'd been envisioning.

She opened the door of the restaurant and spotted Mike immediately at a quiet corner table. He sat facing the door, his attention on everyone who walked in. When he saw her and smiled, her pulse leaped in response. She was definitely playing with fire to have even agreed to this dinner, she realized. But she was here, and she had a mission—to find out whether Ernie had suggested this alternate plan for her cutter—or Mike. She crossed to the table.

"You look terrific," he said.

"Thanks." She had to admit she enjoyed his admiration of her outfit almost as much as she'd hated Colby's.

"Did you get rid of the sleaze from Chicago?"

"I'll tell you about that in a minute. But I have an idea. Before visiting hours are over at TMC, why don't we give your dad a call and see how he's doing? I'm sure Janice over at the art gallery will let us use the phone, and I'll just settle the charges with her later."

"I called him before I walked down here. He's doing fine."

"Oh." She hadn't counted on Mike being so dutiful.

"But you're welcome to call him before we order, if you want."

"Maybe...maybe I will. Do you happen to have the

number handy?" She could call without arousing his suspicion, she decided. After all, she was practically a daughter to Ernie.

"Sure. I carry it around with me these days." He took his wallet from his back pocket, pulled a slip of paper from it and handed it to her.

"Thanks," she said. "I'll be right back."

"How about if I order us a bottle of wine while I'm waiting for you?"

"Okay." She couldn't very well tell him not to. He had a right to drink wine with his meal if he wanted. But she'd be wise not to have more than a small glass of it herself, especially after seeing that telltale circle imprinted on the leather of his wallet. Maybe he always carried condoms. Maybe this particular one had nothing to do with their dinner date. But she wasn't taking any chances.

"What do you like?" he asked.

"I've become partial to a good merlot."

He grinned at her. "I'd be willing to splurge on champagne."

"Not on your life." Her heart beat faster at his teasing reference to the champagne punch they'd both been drinking the night of the rehearsal dinner. "It's nearly eight. I'd better go call."

"Go ahead. The merlot and I will be waiting."

Damned if he wasn't flirting with her, she thought as she left the restaurant and walked next door to the art gallery. And damned if she didn't like it far too much.

Janice was busy with an older couple when Beth entered the gallery, but she looked up long enough for Beth to pantomime using the phone. Janice nodded and Beth went back into the gallery's small office. Janice kept the gallery open on summer evenings to entice whatever tourists were in town, and she'd advised Beth to do the same with her gift shop. So far Beth had resisted because she used her evenings to create new designs and she needed solitude for that.

She consulted the number written in Mike's angular handwriting and dialed.

Ernie picked up the phone on the second ring. "Hello?" He sounded completely worn-out.

Remorse washed over her at the thought that she'd woken him up. "It's Beth. I hope you weren't asleep."

"Who can sleep in a place like this?" His tone brightened considerably. "Where're you calling from, sweetpeach?"

"Janice's gallery. Mike's next door at Café Roca. We're having dinner together."

"Are you? That rascal didn't mention you two were having dinner. That's nice, Beth. Real nice. Is that why you called? To tell me that?"

"Not exactly. I just wanted to wish you a good night's rest," she said, "and let you know that Mike seems to think he'll be able to start on the cutter manufacturing tomorrow."

"That's great."

She didn't notice any hesitation in his reply, so maybe it had been Ernie's idea to throw Mike into the breach. "I was surprised he agreed to do it, to be honest. Won't he get bored after a while?"

"He might, but he has more grit than you give him credit for. I wouldn't have asked him if I thought he'd up and leave in the middle. He'll stick it out, Beth. It wouldn't hurt for you to give him some encouragement now and then, a'course."

"What sort of encouragement?"

"You know. Just let him know he's doin' a good job.

He seems to think you don't have a very good opinion of his abilities. You mean a lot to him. Always have."

Her heart beat faster. "He told you that?"

"In a manner of speakin'. And, Beth, don't be bitin' him no more, okay? Anybody'd think you two were still kids, actin' that way."

"Ernie!" She thanked heaven she was in a secluded office where no one could see the color of her face.

"Just had to say my piece, since your dad ain't here to say it. Now go back and enjoy your dinner. They gave me somethin' to help me sleep, and it's startin' to kick in."

Beth took a shaky breath. "Sleep well, Ernie. Good night." She hung up the phone and leaned against the desk. So now Ernie knew that she'd been close enough to Mike to bite him on the lip. She put her hands to her hot cheeks. With luck, she, Ernie and Mike would be the only people in the world who would ever know that.

ERNIE LAY BACK on the pillow and closed his eyes against the pain. He was trying to get by on fewer injections, and it wasn't easy. But he wanted to stay sharp, and the damned injections turned his brain to mush. Mike and Beth would never know what it cost him to act as if he was feeling great whenever either of them came to visit. He even had his favorite nurse Judy fooled a little bit. But he hated being treated as if he were a sick old man.

He took a long, shaky breath that hurt like hell. "You there, Pete?"

Yeah, I'm here, you macho idiot. Call the nurse and get yourself a shot. You aren't proving anything to anybody.

"Look, who's handling this crisis, you or me?"

Handling, hell. You're white as a sheet. You can't be any help to those kids if you're doubled up in pain.

"Never mind that. Do you think I did the right thing, bringing up that biting business?"

Laughter filled the room. *If you must know, it took me back to the old days. I'd forgotten that Beth was the biter in the crowd. Alana and Mike were the hitters, but Beth couldn't hit worth a damn, especially when she was only four and they were both six, so she'd latch onto one of them with her teeth if she thought it was called for.*

"Well, it appears she's still doin' it."

Maybe Mike deserved it.

"Aw, you always did stick up for those girls. They were as tough as my boy, let me tell you. Anybody who claims girls are the weaker sex should've seen those two in action."

And it's still a battle of wills, apparently.

"We'll see. They're out to dinner. Maybe it'll turn out nice for them."

I can't believe it'll be that easy. One dinner isn't going to change everything.

"Yeah, I know. That's why I gotta cut down on those injections. When the time comes that they're at sixes and sevens with each other, I gotta be alert, Pete."

Tell you what. I'll see what I can do. Maybe, if I pull a few strings up here, the people in charge will let me talk to my girls.

"They ain't ever let you before, right?"

Right.

"Then don't strain yourself. You're supposed to be re-tired, now. I've got everything under control."

I wish I could be there, buddy.

"I wish you could, too, Pete." Ernie sighed. "I wish you could, too."

BETH RETURNED TO THE TABLE and slid into her chair opposite Mike. A glass of wine sat at her place and she took a gulp of it.

He watched her with amusement. "Thirsty?"

She stared at the glass in her hand and remembered she'd planned to have very little of the wine. "I guess so." She put down the goblet and picked up her ice water. "Which means I should be drinking this, instead."

"Don't hold back. We have a whole bottle."

"The water tastes good." She held the glass to her cheek as she darted a glance at his lower lip. Sure enough, she could still see the darkened area where she'd bitten him the night before. And Ernie had noticed it, obviously.

"You look flushed," he said. "Everything okay?"

"Sure." She took the glass away again and set it down. She was giving Mike far too many clues about her mental state. "It's just a little warm in here. Ernie's just fine, as you said. He's glad we're having dinner together."

"So you told him?"

"Yes, I told him. Why wouldn't I?"

"Because you seemed so unenthusiastic about this dinner I thought you wouldn't want to advertise the fact that you agreed to share a meal with a bum like me." His off-center smile didn't quite counteract the uncertainty in his eyes.

She thought how easily she'd adopted Colby's evaluation of Mike, which she'd just proven to be false with her phone call to Ernie. Besides that, for two years she'd assumed Mike was indifferent to her father's death, when in fact he'd stayed away in order to spare her and Alana more heartache. Ever since that fateful night eight years ago, she'd been willing to believe the worst about Mike Tremayne, yet except for that incident, he'd never given her reason.

"I don't think you're a bum," she said softly.

"That's—" Mike paused as the waitress arrived to take their order. He glanced at Beth. "Do you know what you want?"

Good question, she thought. *I want you, but I don't want you. It's very confusing.* "The shrimp's my favorite."

"Two of those," Mike said to the waitress as he handed over the menus.

After she left, Mike lifted his glass. "Here's to the Nightingale Cutter. And ridding the town of that anal-retentive jerk from Chicago."

"Uh, he's not gone."

Mike put his glass down. "What do you mean? Didn't you get the two-week extension?"

"Oh, I got that, all right." Beth took a sip of her wine. "But he decided to spend a week of his vacation time in Bisbee. He's staying at a bed-and-breakfast and says he wants to explore the area."

Mike's gaze narrowed. "Huxford's about as likely to vacation in Bisbee as I am to take a job on Wall Street. Either he thinks he can pressure you into changing your mind, or..."

"Or what?"

Mike paused to pick up his wineglass. "Or he's taken a personal interest in you." He drained the glass and set it on the table again. "It's probably both."

"Funny, but he said a similar thing about you."

"Is that right?"

"He said that your...*interest* in me was the only reason you agreed to manufacture the cutter. I told him you were doing it as a favor to your father."

He reached across the table to take her hand. "Then I might as well admit right now that I'm not doing it entirely as a favor for my father."

She foolishly allowed him to keep her hand in his, and the contact zinged up her arm and through her body as if it were wildfire. "Well, of course it's not just for Ernie. You're also doing it to help me launch this new venture, and I appreciate that."

"Okay, I'm doing it for that reason, too, but even that's not all of it." His voice was a low caress. "I'm also doing it because I've been obsessed with you for eight years, and now that I have an excuse to hang around, I'm shamelessly taking advantage of it."

Excitement curled in her stomach, even as a warning voice told her she should pull her hand away and leave the restaurant while she still could resist the temptation he offered. "But I've told you that nothing will happen between us, so you're just wasting your time."

"Could be, and you're probably smart to think that way." He traced the veins on the inside of her wrist with one finger. "There's no guarantee I'll ever be the kind of man you need." He glanced up at her, his eyes warm with desire.

She trembled in reaction to his touch and the look in his eyes. "I know you're not the kind of man I need," she said, although her body was telling her something else.

"You're not willing to consider that I might change?"

She struggled to keep her mental balance. "Mike, reason tells me that you're reacting this way because you need someone familiar around right now, someone to give you a sense of security."

"Do you really believe that's all it is?"

Passion licked at her skin. She swallowed. "This isn't fair."

"I know. I have a hell of a nerve, when I can't promise not to take off the minute my father is out of danger. I've been telling myself all afternoon to find the strength to stay away from you." He looked down at her hand clasped in his, then back up into her eyes. "I can't seem to do it."

"So Colby was right. You just want to get me into bed."

The desire in his eyes hardened into anger and his grip tightened. "No, *Colby* is *not* right. I do care about giving you the chance to make the most of your invention. I also care about giving my father the peace of mind to recover. And as for using the opportunity to get you into bed, that crude phrase is an insult to the way I feel about you."

The urges coursing through her body threatened to destroy her reason. She pulled her hand forcefully from his, grabbed her purse and bolted, thinking only of getting away from him before she fell completely under his spell and did something she'd regret for the rest of her life. He called her name as she dodged through the tables, but she didn't pause even a second.

Once she gained the sidewalk she began to run, but he caught her before she'd gone ten yards. The force of his fingers clamping suddenly over her arm caused her to spin around to face him. Before she could protest, his mouth came down on hers.

She struggled briefly, but the hard, insistent pressure of his kiss soon blotted out everything but raw desire. His tongue thrust deep, and she whimpered as an avalanche of hot passion engulfed her. He plundered her mouth as he held her in an iron grip. Without the strength of his arms holding her upright she would have crumpled to the pavement as her world spun out of control. She'd never encountered such forceful need.

Gasping, he lifted his lips a fraction away from hers. His voice was a hoarse murmur meant only for her ears.

"That's what you're giving up, Beth. It's not the tender scene hanging in your studio window that we're talking about. We're beyond that now." Then slowly he released her and stepped back. There was a drop of blood on his mouth.

"Your lip..."

He touched it again, as he had the night before, and took his hand away to look at the smear of blood. Then he glanced at her. "I guess we shouldn't be afraid of a little blood. After all these years, when we finally do come together, we'll probably have to scratch, and claw, and bite each other just to work everything out between us."

She shook her head. "No," she murmured.

"Yes. But don't worry. It'll be worth a little bloodshed."

"I...I'm going home."

"I'll walk with you."

"No." She backed away as panic set in. "Let me go alone. I have to think."

"This isn't about thinking."

"For me it is." She turned and started back up the street.

"I'll have them send your dinner over," he called softly after her.

"I'm not hungry."

"It can wait until you are hungry." He paused. "And so can I."

6

MIKE NEEDED EVERY OUNCE of self-control he possessed to let Beth walk up the street alone. But he had to do it, just as he'd had to follow her from the restaurant and show her the shattering emotions they could generate before letting her go. Incredible passion lurked in the depths of her soul, and he'd known it, on some level, from the time they were children. Arrogant fool that he was, he considered himself the only man capable of unleashing that passion. He had no right to make love to her, yet in some ways it seemed he was the *only* one who had that right.

He watched until she turned the corner. They'd put on a show for the people strolling down Main Street on this summer night, he thought as he headed back toward the restaurant. He didn't much care, but Beth might. She had to continue living here, doing business here. The saving grace was the character of Bisbee, which tolerated unusual behavior, and sometimes even seemed to encourage it.

Inside the restaurant he ignored curious stares from other diners as he made his way back to the table where their two glasses and the bottle of merlot remained. He was sorry that he'd spoiled their meal together, but not that he'd kissed her that way. It was time she knew.

Their waitress hurried up to him. "Should I serve

your dinners now? I noticed you weren't here, so I held them back."

"You can serve mine. Beth had to leave suddenly. I'd appreciate it if you'd box hers and have someone take it up to her studio."

"I'm sorry, but we don't usually—"

"I'll be happy to pay for the service."

Her glance was assessing. "Okay. I'll see if I can find someone to deliver the meal to Beth. So you'll be dining alone, then?"

"Yes."

"I'll be right out with your dinner." She paused and turned back to him. "You're Mike Tremayne, aren't you?"

"Yep."

"Is it true that you were almost gobbled up by a crocodile? No, not exactly a crocodile, a black something or other."

A reminder of the incident still made the hair on the back of his neck stand up. But he wasn't about to explain the terror of the moment to the waitress. "A black caiman, which is a type of crocodile. A very *old* black caiman," he said with a wink. "If he'd been in his prime, and my friends hadn't been on the ball, we wouldn't be having this conversation. Where'd you hear that, by the way?"

"From your dad. He comes in once in awhile, and he always tells me stories about you. I was sure sorry about him getting sick. How's he doing?"

"Better."

"That's good. Tell him Cindy says hi."

"I'll do that. Thanks." After he sat down, Mike retrieved his wallet from his hip pocket and took out the slip of paper with the hospital phone number on it. Using a stub of a pencil he kept in another pocket, he wrote *Cindy* on the slip of paper. With worrying about his dad and obsessing about Beth, his memory wasn't great these days, but he didn't want to forget the greeting from Cindy. Anything positive that would make Ernie smile was a plus.

He stared at the hospital phone number and longed for the day he wouldn't have to carry it around. If he could just get his dad home again, if he could just see him tending his beloved rose garden or watching a ball game on TV, then perhaps this oppressive feeling of dread would lift.

As Mike put the slip of paper away, he glanced at the circled impression the condom had made on the leather. Not just that particular condom, of course—the groove had been edged by many over the life of the wallet. His travels weren't always in the vicinity of a drugstore, and he had no desire to father a child in the middle of the jungle. He grimaced. Beth had probably noticed it when he'd given her the hospital phone number and concluded that he planned to seduce her tonight.

He'd had no such plan. He'd hoped they might take a walk up the winding narrow streets to enjoy the warmth of the night breeze. A few stolen kisses would have been nice, but that's as far as he'd intended to take things. But he hadn't been able to play it cool when she started in about Colby Huxford. One hint that the jerk was interested in Beth, and Mike felt the possessive snarl of a jaguar ripple his throat. Maybe he'd internalized more of the jungle's primitive laws than he thought.

Cindy arrived with his dinner and he thanked her.

"I've found a kid to deliver Beth's dinner," she said. "It'll cost you five dollars, though."

"Just put it on my bill."

"Ernie told me about the time you swam through a school of piranhas, too."

Mike smiled at her. "You know how it is. You try to make the stories interesting when you write home."

"So you didn't really do that?"

"Well, I did, but the natives do it all the time. The trick to swimming near piranhas is not to be bleeding anywhere."

Cindy's eyes were wide. "I guess Bisbee must seem pretty dull by comparison, huh?"

Mike thought about the past twenty-four hours visiting his father and navigating his relationship with Beth. Funny how his death-defying adventures faded in importance. "Not so far."

"Well, I've lived here all my life, and *I* sure think it's dull."

"So did I when I was your age. But it's a nice town. You're lucky to have grown up here."

She rolled her eyes. "That's what my *parents* say." Then she surveyed the table. "Do you need anything else? More water? Another bottle of wine?"

Although getting smashed had some appeal under the circumstances, Mike decided against it. "This'll be fine."

"Okay. If you need anything more, just let me know."

"Thanks."

She left the table and returned to the kitchen.

As Mike poured himself another glass of wine and began to eat, he thought about the waitress, who seemed so very young to him. It was a shock to realize she wasn't much younger than he'd been when he left Bisbee, and he'd imagined himself to be a real man back then.

"I'm surprised to see you eating alone."

Mike glanced up to the unwelcome sight of Colby Huxford standing beside the table, snappy blazer and all. The guy had to be sweating buckets under that jacket, Mike thought.

"Mind if I sit down?" Huxford asked.

Mike minded a whole lot, but decided not to make an issue of it. He'd already caused enough commotion in this restaurant for one evening. Still, he didn't have to be overly gracious. "Suit yourself."

"Thanks." Huxford lowered himself to the seat and glanced at the half-full wineglass left by Beth. "Looks as if you had some company at one time."

Mike put down his fork. "What do you want, Huxford?"

"Dinner, eventually. I asked around and the consensus seemed to be that this was a good spot. I had planned to have Beth choose the place tonight, but unfortunately she'd made other plans and couldn't have dinner with me."

"Too bad."

Huxford shrugged, causing the shoulder pads in his jacket to slide a little. "No matter. I'll be here all week. There'll be another time."

"Don't count on it."

Huxford turned the wineglass by its stem. "Are you warning me off, Tremayne? Because if you are, save your breath. In addition to asking about places to eat, I asked about you. Seems you're some sort of thrill-seeker who would much rather paddle a dugout down the Amazon than hang around Bisbee, Arizona."

Mike's jaw clenched. "Well, I happen to be here now."

"So what?"

"So stay away from Beth."

"I don't think you're in a position to tell me that. Once

you've failed to produce the cutters in sufficient quantity, I'm quite sure you'll take off for Brazil, leaving Beth's dream in pieces. I intend to be around to put it back together."

"If I believed for one minute that you're capable of that, I'd be happy for her. But I don't believe you'd put her dream back together, Huxford. I believe you'd take advantage of her vulnerability to make money for your company, all the while trying to convince Beth that you're a swell guy. Fortunately she's a smart lady. She might be forced to accept your offer, but she'll never accept you, my friend."

"I think you're wrong."

"And I think you've overstayed your visit to my table. Go find your own."

Huxford pushed the wineglass away and stood. "I'd love to know why she didn't stay for dinner."

The guy was just itching to get punched, but Mike wasn't going to oblige him. Not tonight, anyway. He stared at Huxford until the other man finally shrugged again and walked away.

"Who was *that?*" Cindy asked as she approached with a coffeepot in one hand.

"Nobody important," Mike said.

THE BELL HANGING over the front door of Nightingale's Daughter jingled at eleven-thirty the next morning. Beth took off her safety glasses and put down the piece of emerald glass she'd been grinding on her wheel. If the bell signaled customers, it would only be the second batch that day. Business had been really slow.

Dusting off her hands, she walked into the gift shop to find Colby standing there with a sack filled with what smelled like sandwiches. At least she wouldn't starve in the next week, she thought, with two men insisting on feeding her every time she turned around.

"Lunchtime," Colby said with a grin. Apparently the casual atmosphere of Bisbee had influenced him. He wore slacks and a polo shirt, which might have been chosen because the horizontal stripes of the shirt minimized the fact that he had a narrow chest and shoulders, as she'd suspected all along.

"You really didn't have to do this," she said.

"I know, but you said you'd be too busy to show me around town, so I extrapolated from that and decided you might be too busy to grab some lunch for yourself. So, I brought sandwiches." He glanced around. "Is there somewhere we can eat these?"

That settled the question of whether he planned to drop the sandwiches off, Beth realized. But then she hadn't really expected him to miss an opportunity to hang around. "I have a table in the back we can use," she said.

"Great." He followed her through the louvered double doors behind the counter.

Inviting him into her work area didn't thrill her, but she couldn't have him spread out the sandwiches on one of her display tables or on the counter. The workroom, however, was the place she didn't allow negative feelings to intrude. Colby had a knack for producing negative feelings in her.

"So this is where the magic happens," he said, glancing around as he placed the sandwich bag on the small table she indicated.

"I guess you could say that." She moved to a compact refrigerator in a corner and opened the door. "I have mineral water, several kinds of soft drinks and beer," she said.

"A beer sounds good." He walked over to her light table and began studying the current project taking shape there, a Southwestern-themed window for a dentist's office in Tucson.

She restrained an impulse to throw a sheet over it. Instead she pulled a beer and a cola from the refrigerator and handed the beer to Colby.

"This is very intricate," he said, gazing at the design of a desert landscape containing several different types of cactus in bloom.

"You sound surprised." There it was, his ability to create negative emotions with the inflection in one simple statement. Beth worked to diffuse her irritation. She had a full afternoon ahead of her, and she didn't want Colby to screw it up.

"I'm really not surprised. You're a very talented lady." He walked over and pulled out one of the two chairs at the small oak table.

When he did, Beth understood more fully why she didn't want him sitting there. That was the chair her father had used, and she'd always sat in the other one when they'd taken a break. When she'd become of legal age to drink, they'd occasionally celebrated a particularly successful project with a beer. But she couldn't very well toss Colby out of the chair. He still might be the one who'd save her if Mike didn't come through.

"Pastrami on whole wheat and corned beef on rye," Colby said, taking out the sandwiches. "Take your pick."

"I'll—" Beth paused as the bell over her front door jingled again. "Let me see if that's a customer."

"Sure thing. I'll just wait here for you."

"Go ahead and start eating," she said as she headed

out of the room. She wanted this little lunch over as soon as possible.

"I'll wait," Colby said.

As a reflex Beth closed the double doors behind her as she walked into the gift shop.

Mike stood there, boxes of cutters stacked in his arms and a sack that looked similar to Colby's sitting on top.

Her heart slammed into high gear at the sight of him. As his knowing gaze moved over her, she quivered as if he'd actually taken her in his arms. She ran her tongue over her lips, and the heat in his glance intensified.

"I heard voices," he said, his voice husky in the stillness. "Do you have company back there?"

"Colby brought over sandwiches."

Irritation flickered in his eyes. "Funniest thing. So did I." He walked over to the counter and deposited his burden.

As he did, Beth noticed he'd shifted to typical Bisbee dress—shorts and a T-shirt. The leather thong attached to the jaguar tooth was tucked inside the neck of the shirt. She found herself admiring the way the shirt fit and gazing at the strong, tanned length of his calves before catching herself and returning her scrutiny to the cutter boxes stacked on the counter. "You've had a busy morning."

"Got up early. Couldn't sleep."

She glanced away from his penetrating stare. She hadn't slept much, either, and she'd been working on the dentist's window since six. "Any problems?" she asked.

"With the cutters? No. With my concentration? A few. But I toughed it out."

"I'll call UPS and have these shipped out today," she said.

"Don't you want to check them over?"

She looked into his eyes. "Are they okay?"

"Yes."

"Then I don't have to check them over. Thanks, Mike."

"I may not get quite as many done this afternoon. I'm interviewing a guy from Sierra Vista who's a good candidate to train as an assistant. It means lost time now, but better production in the long run."

"My God, you're sounding like a businessman."

He grinned, easing the tension between them. "Scary, isn't it?"

"Really scary." For a moment, as they exchanged glances, it was like being back in high school again, teasing each other in the hallways between classes. Beth felt a tug of nostalgia. Then she remembered Colby sitting in her workroom. "Listen, about the sandwiches—"

"I take it you have a good supply already."

She regretted Colby's arrival more than she could say. Mike sitting in her workroom would have been a pleasure. A temptation, but a pleasure, nevertheless. "Well, I—"

"Never mind." He took the sandwiches from the stack of boxes. "I need to get back, anyway."

"Thanks for bringing over the cutters."

"No problem." He lowered his voice. "Tell me something. Is he wearing a damned sport coat today?"

She stifled a laugh. "No. I guess the heat got to him so he's wearing a polo."

"I didn't know they made polo shirts with shoulder pads."

"You're terrible." She met Mike's glance and the laughter threatened to erupt. "And you'd better go."

"Yeah. Listen, want to ride with me up to see Dad tonight?"

She sobered immediately. A trip to Tucson with Mike was probably more intimate than she could handle. "That's okay. I'll just drive up myself."

"My rental car has air-conditioning."

"You do know how to tempt a girl."

"I'll behave myself. And for old times' sake, I'll buy you a DQ in Benson on the way."

"Oh, Mike." She'd never forgotten those special outings to Tucson—her father and Ernie in the front seat, the three kids piled in the back. A stop in Benson at the local Dairy Queen had been one of the sacred rituals.

"I'll pick you up at five." Grabbing the sandwich bag, he left before she could frame a reply, let alone an excuse.

She made a quick call to schedule a UPS pickup and returned to the workroom.

"Did you sell anything?" Colby asked.

She noticed he'd helped himself to a second beer. "No. It was Mike, dropping off the first batch of cutters for me to ship out this afternoon." She sat down and picked up a sandwich, not even caring which one she chose.

"So you like corned beef, do you?"

She forced herself to be polite. "It's just fine. Thanks, Colby."

"Speaking of Tremayne, I ran into him last night."

That got her attention, but she kept her gaze on her sandwich. "Oh, really?"

"I must have walked into Café Roca soon after you left. He was still there."

She cursed the warmth that climbed to her cheeks. "I—couldn't stay. I had some work to do."

"He told me to keep away from you."

Beth almost choked on her sandwich. She swallowed and took a drink of her soda to buy some time before responding with a glance at Colby. She decided to try playing dumb. "Mike's always had a big brother complex where I'm concerned. He must have some crazy idea you have a personal interest in me."

Colby leaned back in his chair. "Why is that so crazy?"

"Because once this is all settled, one way or the other, you'll go back to Chicago and I'll stay here. There's no future in a personal relationship between us, and you might as well know that I don't believe in casual flings."

"Neither do I."

She'd bet next month's studio rent that he was lying. Colby was exactly the type to believe in one-night stands. A little voice in the back of her mind whispered that unfortunately, so was Mike.

"We're in a wonderful new age, Beth." Colby paused to take another drink of his beer. "Handmade is headquartered in Chicago, but it has representatives all over the country who report in by phone, fax and e-mail. I've chosen to stay in the main office because I grew up in Chicago and I've never had a reason to leave. But with all the traveling I do with the company, I could live anywhere I wanted and still do my job just fine."

"Aren't you getting a little ahead of yourself? We haven't even had a date, yet."

"That isn't because I haven't tried." He gestured toward the table. "We can count this as a date, for that matter."

"No, I don't think we can." She balled up the rest of her sandwich and shoved it into the bag. "Because the truth is, I'm not interested in a personal relationship with you." She met his gaze. "If that means we can't work together on the cutter, then I'm sorry. And if you're staying in Bisbee in hopes that I'll change my mind, I'm afraid you're wasting your time."

He looked unperturbed by her announcement. "I hope you're not saving yourself for Tremayne."

"No, I'm not." She stood. "And I really need to get those cutters ready to ship, if you'll excuse me."

"He told me last night that if I'd take good care of you, he'd be happy for you."

A pulse beat at her temple, signaling an oncoming headache. "I thought you said he told you to stay away from me?"

"He did, but that was because he probably views me the same way you do, a one-night-stand type. I didn't bother to explain the details of my job flexibility to him, because frankly, it's none of his damn business. I'm only pointing out to you that if he thought I'd do right by you, he'd abandon the field to me, because he's not the slightest bit interested in sticking around."

"I know that." Which she did, but hearing it coming from Colby made the truth sound all that much worse. "And I have no intention of getting involved with either of you."

He stood and picked up the sandwich bag. "All I'm saying is that I'm a better bet than he is."

"I'm not in a betting mood these days."

"That's okay." He shoved his empty beer cans into the sack. "Because I am."

Normally she would have asked him to leave the empty cans because she recycled them, but the global environment didn't matter as much as the environment in her studio at the moment, and she wanted all signs of him gone. "Goodbye, Colby. Thanks for the sand-wiches."

"You're welcome." He left the workroom and contin-ued through the gift shop to the front door. "See you to-morrow," he called over his shoulder just before he left.

She swore under her breath. She didn't want to see him tomorrow, or the day after. In fact, she was tempted to tell him she'd never sign a lease agreement with Handmade and certainly would never fall in with his personal plans, so he might as well take off.

As she turned on the computer in a corner of the workroom and started printing mailing labels for the cutter boxes, she thought about her predicament. Saying she wouldn't sign the agreement because she disliked Colby Huxford would be cutting off her nose to spite her face, as her father used to say. And she desperately wanted this cutter to be a success so that an invention her father hadn't lived long enough to put into produc-tion would become everything he and Ernie had dreamed it could be.

No, she had to humor Colby along without giving him any encouragement whatsoever that she'd like a more personal involvement. And she'd be wise to take the same approach with Mike, although that would require more willpower. A *lot* more willpower. She'd spent her nights in an agony of sexual frustration.

Once the labeling was finished, she returned to her cutting table. Instantly she felt the prickly sensation of Colby's remembered presence in the workroom. Deter-mined to shake it off, she picked up the piece of amber glass she'd chosen for a section of the dentist's window, laid it over the pattern and positioned the cutting wheel. It was an expensive piece of glass, but it gave the effect she wanted. Applying pressure to the wheel, she started to follow the lines of the pattern. The glass cracked.

She took a deep breath and consciously unclenched her jaw. Then she took a fresh piece of glass and tried again. Again it cracked.

"Dammit!" She walked away from the table. One thing was for sure. Colby was not setting foot in her workshop again.

7

MIKE COULD TELL Beth hadn't had a good afternoon from her expression as she got into the car. He congratulated himself on noticing her expression at all considering the fact that for the trip into Tucson she'd changed into a scoop-necked red T-shirt tucked into white shorts. He forced himself not to ogle at the creamy expanse of thigh only inches away from his hand as he fiddled with the radio dial trying to find some tunes to serenade them on the way out of town.

"Forget it until we get closer to Tucson," she said as they drove up Tombstone Canyon and headed toward the Time Tunnel.

He switched off the radio. "Just thought some music might cheer you up."

She glanced at him, her eyes hidden behind wire-framed sunglasses. "How do you know I'm not cheered up?"

"Your mouth gets all tight when you're upset."

"My mouth isn't tight."

"Yes, it is."

"Is not." She pulled on her lower lip and made a face at him.

He laughed. "Now it's not."

"It's all that damned Colby's fault. He insisted on eating lunch in my workroom, and after he left I couldn't cut glass without breaking it."

Mike's gut tightened. "He didn't try anything, did he?"

"Like what?"

"You know what. I swear if he ever touches you, I'm going to rearrange his face."

"Thanks, but I think I can take care of myself in that department." She paused. "He mentioned meeting you at Café Roca last night."

He glanced over at her. She was staring straight ahead at the two-lane highway. "Yeah, he slithered over to my table wearing his ever-present sport coat."

"According to him, you said if he'd do right by me, you'd be happy."

Mike groaned. Apparently it was his lot in life to be misunderstood, especially when it came to Beth. "That's not quite how it went."

"Then how did it go?"

"He claimed I'd fail at this cutter production and leave you with your dreams shattered. He said he'd be on hand to help put your dream back together. I said if I truly believed an association with him would be good for you, I'd be happy for you. I just don't happen to believe it."

"So let me get this straight. If the right guy came along, you'd turn me over to him with your blessing? You'd send us postcards from the depths of the jungle, and when you came home for visits you'd bring our kids exotic trinkets from the rain forest and ask them to call you Uncle Mike? Is that what you're saying?"

His stomach churned at the thought of somebody else marrying Beth and fathering her children. But what else could he expect if he remained committed to his explorations in Brazil? "I want you to be happy."

"That's not exactly an answer to the question."

"Yeah, sure. I'd be thrilled to see you hooked up with a terrific guy," he lied.

"That's not true, Mike. That little muscle is jumping in your jaw."

"So what?"

"So that's how I always knew when you didn't really mean what you were saying. You know what I think you'd like?"

"I have a feeling you're about to tell me."

"I think you'd like me to be your secret lover with no strings attached on your part, and when you're off in the jungle somewhere, you'd expect me to be true to you."

Exactly. He was ashamed of how accurately the description fit his fantasy. "What kind of guy would expect a one-sided deal like that?"

"I'm not saying you'd have the nerve to ask it of me. I'm just saying that's what you'd like, if you could get away with it."

He sighed and stretched his arms out against the steering wheel. His shoulders were knotted up from spending long hours at a workbench, and he longed for something that would involve big muscle movement. Making love to Beth would be perfect, but he didn't anticipate that happening in the near future. "I guess any guy would want a deal like that, if he could get away with it," he finally admitted.

"Well, here's a news flash for you, Mike. These are the nineties, and you can't get away with it."

He sent her a tired grin. "Can't blame a man for trying." He rolled his shoulders a couple of times.

"Pull over for a minute and let me work those kinks out before you get so tight you can't even drive."

He didn't have to be asked twice. He found a wide spot next to the road and parked the sedan, although he left the engine running so they could still have air-conditioning.

Beth unhooked her seat belt. "Take off your seat belt and turn your back toward me."

He followed her instructions and soon her strong hands began exploring the source of his pain.

"You're tensed up something awful," she said, rotating the heel of her hand under his shoulder blade. "You shouldn't have tried to do so much the first day."

"I took a look at that list of back orders and decided I couldn't just ease into it." He groaned as she pushed her thumb against a particularly tender spot.

"You'll be no good to me if you're crippled up."

"A little more of this and I'll be fine. But if you're offering to give me another massage tomorrow night, I accept. You're wonderful at it."

"Strong hands come naturally when you cut glass all day."

He leaned into the massage and sighed with relief as his tortured muscles began to relax. "Mmm. That's great."

He noticed she'd stopped talking.

"Yeah, right there," he murmured, thinking she might need the encouragement. Still she made no response, although the massage became more vigorous. She really was good at this, he thought. He could get used to it.

"God, that's good, Beth," he said on a heartfelt sigh.

Abruptly the massage ended.

He turned to her in surprise. She had her head down and she was fumbling with her seat belt.

"All done?"

"Yep." She didn't look at him.

He took note of her rosy cheeks and tilted her chin up. "Beth?"

The look of pure desire in her eyes told him all he needed to know about her state of mind. With a moan he pulled her close and sought the honeyed depths of her mouth. Her response was instantaneous as she clutched the back of his head and urged him deeper. But he couldn't seem to get enough of her. He kept seeking a different angle for greater penetration as he reveled in her explosion of passion.

The console was a frustrating barrier to the full contact he craved, but the separation of their bodies gave him access to the lush curve of her breast straining against her T-shirt. He cupped the weight of her breast through the soft material, and she moaned, pressing the tight bud of her nipple against his thumb. It was all the encouragement he needed to tug the shirt from the waistband of her shorts and reach underneath to flip the catch on her bra. At last he caressed the silken warmth of her skin, skimming his palm up her rib cage until he cradled her breast. His heartbeat drumming in his ears and his groin aching, he kneaded the soft flesh and rejoiced in her shuddering breath.

A car whizzed past and the wind from its passage rocked the car.

She placed her hands on either side of his jaw and eased away from his mouth. "We...have...to stop," she whispered raggedly.

He teased her nipple with his thumb as he lifted his head and gazed into her eyes. "Or find a lonelier road."

She grew still, and the flame of desire in her eyes began to cool. "I guess that's your style, isn't it?" She shrugged out of his embrace and pulled her shirt down. "For all I know, we aren't very far from the back road where you tried to seduce Alana the night before the wedding."

"Hey." Frustration fueled his anger. He was very close to telling her that her precious older sister had lied about that. "Don't get bitchy with me. I didn't start this."

"Excuse me, but I don't believe I was the one who grabbed you." She reached behind her back with both hands to refasten her bra.

Watching her arch her back to do it, which caused her chest to be thrust in his direction, made him almost crazy. "No, you were the one so turned on by giving me a massage you almost couldn't stand it! I'd like to meet the man who wouldn't make a move when you give him a look like the one you gave me a few minutes ago. If you're really not going to let this go further, then stop looking at me like that."

She tucked her shirt back into her shorts and took a deep breath. "I shouldn't have agreed to come on this trip with you."

"I'd willingly take you back, but that's going to make me late to see my dad. He's expecting me at a certain time and it's important that I be there."

She stared down at her hands clenched in her lap. "I don't want to mess that up, either. Let's go."

He buckled his seat belt and put the car in gear.

After they'd traveled several more miles down the road, she spoke. "You're absolutely right. I'm sending you mixed signals, because that's what I am, mixed-up. I wish I could be more like you."

"What's that supposed to mean?"

She lifted her head, and her gaze was tortured. "Why do I have to want more than sexual satisfaction? With you it's simple, just like the natives of the rain forest— make love when we have the opportunity and part with no regrets. Why can't I look at it that way? And you're right about something else, too. Alana would never have to know."

"No, she wouldn't, but..."

"But what?"

Oh, great, now he was having an attack of conscience, just when she was trying to make his case for him. "But I don't want you to do anything that would go against your beliefs. If making love to me would gnaw at you for the rest of your life, if you wouldn't be able to look Alana in the eye again, then you shouldn't do it, no matter how good it might feel at the time." And it would feel damned good, he thought, glancing at her sitting there beside him. He must be out of his mind to be shoring up her defenses instead of tearing them down with both hands.

A hint of a smile touched her lips. "Is that some kind of reverse psychology, Mike?"

"God help me, it's the way I feel. You know how much I want you, and you even have some idea of what it could be like between us. If I really thought you could enjoy making love to me with no regrets, we wouldn't even bother driving back to Bisbee after seeing my dad. We'd check right into a hotel. But you're not put together that way, and I'm finally realizing it."

"A hotel?"

Hearing the breathless note in her voice nearly finished him. "Don't push it, Beth." He switched on the radio and found a station he could live with—soft rock and pop.

"Alana's calling again tomorrow morning to check on Ernie's progress."

The statement hung between them for several long seconds. "Are you going to tell her I'm here this time?" he asked finally.

"You said once before that I should tell her and let her decide what she wants to do about it."

"I didn't actually say you should tell her. I just think that if you do, she's the one responsible for her actions if she decides to come back."

Beth was silent for a while. "If she does come home while you're here, are you planning to say anything about your feelings for me?"

"That's up to you." He looked at her. "But personally I think it's time we got this all out in the open."

Her voice was almost too low to hear above the radio. "If she thinks you care for me instead of her, she might hate me."

His heart ached for her. Reaching for the volume knob, he turned down the radio. "I can't believe that she would," he said gently. "She might be upset at first, but she loves you, Beth. Ultimately she'd want you to be happy."

"And would I be happy, Mike?"

The question hit him hard. What did he think he was doing, asking her to risk her heart and her relationship with her sister for some guy who wouldn't make promises? "Maybe not. Maybe I'd better keep my damn mouth shut, and after my dad's out of the woods, I'll just leave town again."

She didn't respond to that.

As they reached the outskirts of Benson, he cleared his throat. "Still want that ice cream?"

"Sure. Why not?"

"Why not, indeed."

"I hope they still have butterscotch dipped cones."

"How long since you've been there?"

"Too long." She moved her seat back and stretched out her legs.

He kept his attention on the road and away from her slender legs with great difficulty.

After a while Beth spoke again. "You know, there was a special feeling in the air during those years when the five of us were always doing things together. Life was just plain fun most of the time."

"Pete and Ernie were a great combination. What one didn't come up with, the other one did."

"I miss the excitement of those times, Mike." She glanced at him. "I suppose they don't seem so exciting, considering what you've experienced down in South America."

"My adventures were a different kind of excitement." He was beginning to think that knocking around the Amazon jungle for eight years had been an effort to replace that sense of excitement and wonder that he'd had growing up with Pete and Ernie and the girls around to make things interesting. Surely not. Life in a small town would be boring to him now, wouldn't it? So why was he so looking forward to the relatively simple pleasure of a Dairy Queen?

The ice cream shop, located right next to the main road going through Benson, was busy. Mike scored a parking spot by staying alert, and they left the windows down so the car interior wouldn't heat up while they were buying their cones.

The atmosphere inside the Dairy Queen's small service area was pure summer, with sunburned people in shorts and flip-flops crowding into the space, debating their choices as they stared up at the array of treats displayed in sun-faded Technicolor on the back wall. Mike thought of all the native children he'd met who had never tasted ice cream. With luck they never would, because that would mean their simple way of life had been destroyed.

But Mike wasn't truly of their world, and when the freckle-faced kid behind the window handed a butter-scotch-dipped cone to Beth and a chocolate-dipped one to him, he experienced a moment of déjà vu, and it felt good. Then another thought came to him, completely unbidden. He wondered what it would feel like to bring his own kid here. Now he'd *never* considered something like that before. Oddly enough, the idea didn't panic him the way he might have expected it would.

"Let's sit out on the picnic table and eat these." He remembered that's what Ernie and Pete had always suggested, probably to save the seat covers.

"Do we have time?"

"With the temperature what it is outside, we'll have to eat these puppies in twenty seconds flat or they'll be soup. I think we have time."

When Beth and Mike walked outside, a family with two little children, a boy about four and a girl about three, were just leaving the picnic table in a shady spot next to the ice cream shop. While Mike bit off the top section of his cone he watched the family. The kids skipped around the parents, who were holding hands and laughing as they dodged the children's game of tag. It was a sweet scene, and Mike watched it with uncharacteristic longing as he took a seat on one side of the old wooden picnic table.

"Mike, you're dripping."

He looked at his cone and sure enough, a white river was running from underneath the chocolate layer over the lip of the cone and down between his fingers. He turned the cone sideways and sucked out the melting ice cream before licking the ice cream from his fingers.

"Do you know those people?" Beth asked.

He glanced across the table at her. She was busily attending to her own cone, and the action of her pink tongue and full lips was so unknowingly provocative that the material of his shorts tightened over his straining erection once again. "No, I don't know them. They just looked like a nice family."

Beth watched the four people get into a minivan and pull out into traffic. "I wonder what it would have been like to have a mother around."

"Nice, I guess." He glanced at her while he continued to eat his cone as quickly as possible. She would make a terrific mother—creative, empathetic, firm without being bossy. Any kid would be lucky to end up with her as a mom. He pictured a couple of little kids sitting beside her, eating their cones and getting the ice cream on their noses and their chins. He smiled.

"What's that for?" She'd reduced the swirl of ice cream to a cylindrical mound that stuck up over the edge of the cone by about two inches. All the butterscotch was gone.

"Oh, nothing."

"You'd better watch out. When people start grinning for no reason the guys in white coats come after them with butterfly nets." Then she took the mound of ice cream in her mouth.

Mike was transfixed by the image. In fact, the image gave him definite pain in the lower reaches of his body. He must have let out a little growl of male anticipation, because she looked up at him, a question in her eyes.

Then she glanced down at his cone. "Flash flood, Mike."

"Damn." While he'd been lost in a fantasy orgy with

Beth, melted ice cream had covered his hand and dripped all over his shorts.

"Looks like I can't take you anywhere," she said, grinning. "Better go over to the drinking fountain and see if you can clean yourself up."

He did, tossing the cone in the trash can on his way. He had to wait for a couple of boys who were drinking from the old porcelain fountain as if they'd just crossed the Sahara on their hands and knees. The fountain had also been the cleanup spot when he was a kid, he remembered as he finally got his turn and ran his sticky hand under the stream of water. Then he took the bandanna from his pocket, wet it down and began dabbing at the front of his shorts.

Beth came over to watch. "You're a mess. I don't remember you dripping all over yourself like that when you were ten."

Mike kept working away at the spots as the front of his shorts got wetter and wetter. "That's because at ten I had absolutely no imagination."

"No imagination? You were the one who convinced me the drainage ditch near your house had crocodiles in it."

"I mean no imagination about more adult things." He glanced around and lowered his voice. "Like how a cylinder of ice cream could stand for something else, especially when a certain woman you're highly attracted to takes it into her mouth with such skill."

Beth's hoot of laughter bounced off the whitewashed block wall of the Dairy Queen. "You truly are obsessed. That's how I always eat my ice cream cones, and it has no subliminal meaning whatsoever," she said, still chuckling.

"Good practice," he muttered.

"And what makes you think I'd want to practice?"

He stopped dabbing and balled the damp bandanna in one hand as he straightened to look at her. "Because you're one of the sexiest women I've ever known."

"I find that difficult to believe."

"So do I. It's been a revelation to me that little Beth, the girl I spent all those clueless years goofing around with, would turn out to be the one woman who can sexually wrap me around her little finger."

"Could always be the forbidden fruit syndrome."

"I've thought of that. But the way things are going, I'll probably never know."

"And how are things going?"

"You're ready to give in and enjoy the moment just when I'm having a huge attack of conscience about ruining your life forever with my base and greedy nature."

"So that's your evaluation?"

"Am I wrong?"

She adjusted her sunglasses. "I think that huge attack of conscience might have something to do with being scared."

"Scared? Of what?"

"Finding out that you need a woman for more than just sex."

He stared at her in silence while he tried to come up with a convincing denial of that statement. Trouble was, his gut was telling him she could, just possibly, be right.

"Come on." She started for the car. "We'd better get moving if we want to catch Ernie before his sleep medication kicks in."

The radio filled in the lack of conversation between them during the rest of the trip. Mike was busy thinking, and he figured Beth must be, too. Every time he glanced over at her she looked as if she was a million miles away.

The twist she'd put on his motives didn't make him seem like quite the nice guy he'd been telling himself he was.

All this time the emphasis had been on how a physical relationship between them would affect Beth, with the assumption being it wouldn't affect Mike at all. Maybe he'd begun to realize that wasn't true. If it turned out he couldn't live without Beth around, he'd be in a world of hurt. Right now he hadn't established any connections that demanding, so he was free to pursue his life in any way he chose.

What had begun as a simple need to make love to her had become much more complicated. It was quite possible that she possessed the power to completely upend his life as he knew it. He remembered Pete used to say *Be careful what you wish for.* Mike hadn't understood the wisdom in that warning until now.

He found a space in the TMC parking lot and they walked together, not touching, into the building.

As they headed for Ernie's room, Beth spoke for the first time since they'd left Benson. "I didn't bring him anything. I'd meant to get him something to make him laugh, and I—forgot."

"I didn't bring him anything, either," Mike said. "But as far as making him laugh, the ice cream splotches on my shorts should do the trick, don't you think?"

Beth smiled. "Are you planning to tell him how you got in that condition?"

"No, and I'd appreciate it if you'd keep that part of the story to yourself, if you don't mind. We can just say it was very hot and I couldn't eat fast enough."

"What was very hot?" she asked, a mischievous gleam in her eye.

"You're turning out to be a lot of trouble, you know."

"Oh, I do know." Her knowing gaze met his.

"After we see Ernie, we'll talk."

"Okay."

They were only a few yards from Ernie's room when activity erupted from it. A gurney was shoved out and attendants pushed it at a rapid clip down the hall away from them while a physician running behind barked orders.

Mike glanced at Beth in horror and without speaking they took off at a run down the hallway after the gurney. Mike arrived at the hurried procession first.

"That's my dad!" he cried, grabbing the physician by the arm as he reached him. "What's happened?"

"We're taking him to ICU," the doctor said. "Could be a pulmonary embolism."

"You mean a blood clot?"

"That's right."

"Is it serious?"

The doctor glanced at him. "Let's hope not."

8

AS THE WAITING ROOM VIGIL outside the Intensive Care
Unit wore on, Mike realized that Beth's presence was es-
sential to his sanity. They took turns going in to see Ernie
for brief visits, and whenever she left him alone in the
waiting room, he nearly went out of his mind. The doctors had tried to calm his fears by telling him that the in-
travenous drug was dissolving the blood clot in his
dad's lung and he was progressing well. Mike knew that
if the blood clot had been a little larger, it could have
killed his father in seconds. He got the shakes every time
he thought about that. He couldn't lose his dad now.

He and Beth satisfied what little hunger they had from
vending machine snack food and drank countless cups
of coffee. Other people, checking on other patients in
ICU, drifted in and out of the waiting room, but every
group seemed huddled inside its own tragedy, unwilling to strike up conversations with outsiders.

To pass the time, Beth drew him into talking about his
experiences in the rain forest. He knew she was doing it
to distract him, and he was grateful. Somewhere along
the way he found himself describing the encounter with
the black caiman, except this time he didn't pretty it up,
or make jokes as he had in the letter home to his father.

"The zoologist in the party I was guiding wanted to
search out a species of crocodile called caimans, so I took
him out in a boat at night," he said, sitting forward on

the Naugahyde couch and letting his hands hang loose between his knees. "If you shine a flashlight on the water, the iris of a crocodile eye will reflect in it. The smaller ones, the speckled caimans, show up yellow, but the black caimans glow red."

"That's spooky, right there," Beth said. "Looking for red-eyed creatures on a jungle river at night."

"Well, that's how you find them. So we'd located and measured about six of the speckled caimans, which are pretty harmless, when the black caiman showed up in the flashlight beam. From the size of his eyes I figured him to be at least twenty feet long."

"My God."

"Usually the big ones will sink out of sight. They're shy. But this one wasn't moving." He laced his fingers together because they'd begun to tremble slightly. "I told the zoologist we should get the hell out of there, but he ordered me closer so he could measure it." He glanced at her. "That's when the caiman took a hunk out of the boat."

Beth gasped. "How close to you?"

"Too damn close. I dove out. So did the zoologist. We made it to shore while the caiman was busy destroying the boat, along with all the guy's equipment. After it was over I threw up." When she didn't respond to the end of the story, he glanced around at her. Her face was white with strain. Filled with remorse, he took her icy hand in his. "Sorry. I shouldn't have told you that one. Let's get back to one of my monkey stories. One time I—"

"No, Mike. Don't insult me by treating me like a child. Your story may frighten me, but I'm not weak."

"I know you're not." In her eyes he rediscovered the strength that he'd depended on more than he'd realized over the years. "I didn't tell my dad exactly what happened with that monster. I don't think he needs to know the details.''

"I'm glad you chose to tell me."

"So am I." He rubbed her hand to warm it. "I stayed awake all night, thinking. I'd had some close calls, but I'd never thought any of them would kill me. This time was different." He tightened his hold on her hand. "This isn't a line, Beth. I swear it isn't. I thought about you that night."

She held his gaze and her throat moved in a convulsive swallow.

"I thought about my dad, too, and my life so far. I couldn't justify much of it as being worth anything. And the worst part was knowing that if the caiman had killed me, my dad would be the only one who'd care."

"Not the only one."

"I didn't know that." He savored the warmth in her eyes and wondered how she managed to look so damned good after hanging around a waiting room until four in the morning. "I don't know what I would have done without having you here."

Beth gave him a tired smile. "I don't know what I would have done without you here, either. When Ernie had the heart attack, Alana came down from Phoenix, so at least we had each other to lean on." She paused and glanced at her watch. "She's due to call in three hours. If I'm not home yet, she'll just get the answering machine. I have no idea how to reach her."

"It's just as well."

She glanced at him. "In what way?"

He sighed and squeezed her hand. "In all ways. By the time she could get back here, he'll either be out of danger, or…he won't. If he's out of danger soon there's no point in her coming back now. And if he doesn't…get out of danger, then..." He discovered he couldn't finish the sentence. Something seemed to be lodged in his throat.

Beth's hand tightened in his. "He's going to make it."

He returned the pressure of her hand. "Yep. He has to. He just has to."

"Do you think he realizes we drove up here together? I told him, but because they haven't wanted both of us in there at the same time, I don't know if he understood what I was saying."

"He's fuzzy on what's happening, that's for sure." Mike smiled faintly. "Although one of the interns told me they had a hard time getting an oxygen mask on him at first because he wanted to keep his rubber cigar."

Beth stared at him. "His *what?*"

"One of the nurses bought him a fake cigar at a costume shop. It looks pretty damned real. Yesterday morning when I walked in, he had it stuck in the corner of his mouth, just the way he's always had a real one for as long as I can remember. I went ballistic. He got the biggest kick out of my reaction."

Beth leaned her head back on the cushion. "What a guy. When did he notice the bite mark on your lip?"

"He mentioned that to you?"

"Oh, yes."

"When?"

"When I called last night after we met for dinner. He didn't just mention it, either. He lectured me about not doing it again. Shades of our childhood."

Mike leaned his head back next to hers and turned to look into her eyes. "So that's why you seemed all flustered when you came back from the phone call. You knew my dad had found out we'd done more than shake hands since I got home."

"He doesn't miss much, you know."

"Meaning what?"

"Once he's not so doped up, he'll know exactly how things stand between us. All our talk about nobody knowing if we became involved didn't take Ernie into account."

Mike reached up and ran a finger down the bridge of her nose. "According to you, I'm so scared of getting involved with you that nothing's going to happen, so we have nothing to worry about."

She gazed into his eyes. "I could be wrong."

An image of loving her shimmered in his mind. "Indeed you could."

"Mike? Beth?"

They both leaped to their feet at the sound of the doctor's voice. Mike held tight to Beth's hand, while he searched the doctor's face for good news. This guy wasn't big on showing his emotions, but Mike thought he looked cautiously optimistic. Mike held his breath and prayed.

"Everything's looking much better now," the doctor said, clasping his hands in front of him. "We've decided to take him off the IV and put him on oral medication. Pretty soon we should be able to return him to his room. The worst is over."

Mike turned to Beth and swept her into a bear hug, burying his face in her hair to hide the grateful tears that ran down his cheeks. When he finally felt in control of himself enough to release her, he noticed her face was pretty damp, too.

"We'll continue to keep a close watch on him," the doctor said, "but I think it's time for you two to go home and get some sleep. You won't do him any good if you put too much stress on yourselves."

Mike swiped a hand across his face. "Can we both go in now?"

"Sure. Then I strongly recommend you get some rest."

"We'll go see him, and then we'll decide about that," Mike said. Still holding Beth's hand firmly in his, he started toward the doors leading into ICU.

HOLDING FAST TO MIKE, Beth approached the narrow bed where Ernie lay looking pale and exhausted. Beth concentrated on the movement of his chest to reassure herself that he was still alive. His eyes fluttered open. He glanced from Mike to Beth, and even in his drugged state, approval registered in his gaze.

Mike reached for his dad's hand. "You sure raised a ruckus. I'd like it if you wouldn't do that anymore," he said, his voice shaking.

"That goes for me, too," Beth added.

Ernie seemed to be trying to say something.

"Don't try to talk, Dad," Mike said. "I just wanted you to know that Beth hasn't bitten me in two days, now."

"Mike!" Beth cried.

"I appreciate you telling her not to, though," Mike continued. "I guess she still listens to you once in a while, even if I'm the one who has to bribe her with ice cream instead of you."

"He's making all of this up," Beth said, her cheeks warm. But despite her embarrassment, she could see that the teasing had brought a faint sparkle to Ernie's eyes that hadn't been there when he'd first opened them.

"Anyway, we'll be back to see you soon," Mike said. "I love you, Dad. Now get some rest, okay?"

Ernie gave an almost imperceptible nod of his head.

Beth released Mike's hand and moved around him to

brush a quick kiss on Ernie's leathery cheek. "I love you, too," she murmured. "Get better."

Mike recaptured her hand and squeezed it. "We'd better take off. Don't want to overdo it."

"Right." With one last blown kiss to Ernie, she walked with Mike out of the unit.

For a long moment they stared at each other.

Finally Mike reached for her other hand, holding onto both of them as he faced her. "Look, I can't go back to Bisbee. You go. Take the car. I know I'll lose a day at the shop, but I just can't—"

"As if I care about losing a day. I don't want to go back yet, either."

He looked grateful. "You're sure?"

"Hey, he's like a father to me. I could no more drive back to Bisbee right now than fly. But the doctor was right. We probably should get some sleep." She glanced toward the waiting room couches. "Somehow."

His gaze penetrated deep into hers. "There's a hotel a block away. If we leave that phone number the doctor can call us if anything changes. We could be back here almost immediately."

"You're right." Her heartbeat quickened.

He hesitated. "But that's not the only reason I want that hotel room, Beth."

"I know." She gripped his hands very tightly as the need to comfort and take comfort swamped her with powerful force. She loved this man, had always loved him. If he needed her now, she would be there for him.

"Maybe it's wrong to want you right now, but, God help me, I do."

"It's not wrong. It's very human to want to hold someone at a time like this."

His tone roughened. "I don't want to hold just someone. I want to hold you. There's a difference, and I want you to know it."

"I don't really care why you need me, Mike. I just know that you do, and that's enough for me right now. I need to hold you, too."

"But—"

"I don't expect promises. So don't try to think it out. You're the one who said this was about feeling, not thinking."

His sigh was one of surrender. "All right." He released her hands. "I'll go find a telephone and see what they can do for us."

As he walked away, Beth's heart squeezed. He looked more vulnerable than she'd ever known him to be in her life. He was an only kid facing the loss of his only parent. At least she'd always had Alana to cling to. And perhaps, because of Alana, she should feel guilty about the decision she'd just made. But no guilt marred the warm certainty that she was doing what she needed to do at this moment, for herself and for Mike. They'd survived this ordeal together, and nothing seemed more right than taking solace from each other now that it was over.

AS ERNIE DRIFTED OFF to sleep, he heard Pete's voice as plain as day.

What a showoff. You didn't have to pull a stunt like this to get them together, for crying out loud!

Ernie tried to rouse himself enough to answer, but he just didn't have the strength.

Okay, so Mike and Beth are holding hands and depending on each other, but cut out the drama, will you? You're scaring everybody, including me!

Ernie couldn't tell him that the drama was unintentional, but the news that Mike and Beth were holding hands was good. Real good. He smiled.

HAD SHE HAD A CHOICE, Beth would have preferred something other than the impersonal atmosphere of a hotel room when she made love to Mike. But she had no choice. He needed her now, with a ferocity that wouldn't be denied. And she would give him this. Although it could be dangerous to speak words of love, at least she could show him the depth of her feelings.

As he twisted the lock on the door, she pulled the drapes, blocking out the pale beginnings of a new day. The only sound was the soft whisper of an air conditioner and his muted footsteps as he walked toward her.

"I've imagined this hundreds of times," he said gently, "but I always pictured it with you wearing that red dress."

"Let's not talk about that night," she murmured, her heart full of tenderness. "In fact, let's not talk at all."

He reached for her and she snuggled into his arms, into his warmth.

"We have to talk about it," he said, his lips against her forehead.

She hugged him tighter. "No. Not now, Mike."

"Now. Because that was the moment everything began, the moment everything changed."

She grew very still, remembering what he'd said on the street that night in Bisbee. *When we finally do come together, we'll probably have to scratch, and claw, and bite each other just to work everything out between us.*

"That's why you made that circle of glass, isn't it?" he said. "Because that moment changed your life forever, too."

"Mike—"

"Isn't it?" He shoved his fingers through her hair and tipped her head back. "The whole world shifted for you, too. Admit it, Beth."

She gripped his arms so hard her nails imprinted on his skin. "I don't want to talk about that night. I just want to love you, Mike."

"And why don't you want to talk about it?" he persisted as his thumb stroked the line of her jaw.

"You know why."

"Tell me."

She squeezed her eyes shut. He seemed determined to drag them through this swampland. "All right! Because after you kissed me, you tried to make love to her!"

"No, I didn't."

Her eyes flew open. "How dare you deny it." She tried to push him away.

He held her fast and his dark eyes glowed with intensity. "Because I was falsely accused. I didn't try to make love to Alana. She begged me, but I couldn't make love to her after what I'd just found out, that you were the one, you were always the one—"

"No!" She pushed against his chest, her palm coming into contact with the jaguar tooth necklace tucked beneath his shirt. "She told me you did. She told me!"

He wrapped both arms around her and held her tight. "She lied to you, Beth."

She shook her head violently. "She wouldn't do that."

"Not unless she was desperate, and she was. She sensed things were different between us, and she was trying to hang on. I don't blame her for making up that story. I hurt her, and she had to strike out."

No, Beth thought, searching his face for any hint of deception and finding none. Surely Alana wouldn't lie to her, wouldn't deliberately tarnish her image of Mike. "I don't believe you."

"Yes, you do, deep down. I couldn't make love to you without telling you the truth. I don't want Alana's lie between us, poisoning what should be pure and beautiful."

Her voice quivered as she battled with what he was telling her. Believing him meant doubting Alana. But doubting him now would rip her to shreds. "Let me go."

"No." He lowered his head.

"Damn you, let me go!"

"No." His lips hovered over hers. "And I warn you that if you bite me, I'll bite you back."

"I hate you."

"No, you don't. And I'm going to prove it to you." He closed in, taking possession of her mouth, daring to thrust his tongue deep.

She writhed in his arms, trying to get away, but she didn't bite him. She pushed at his chest with both hands, but he only deepened the kiss, probing for the wellspring of desire and love that lay waiting for him, waiting for this moment.

After all the years she'd fought her longing, her capitulation was swift. She'd come to this room to love him. It was, after all, the only thing she wanted. And she knew, in the honesty of his passion for her, that he was telling her the truth about that night. With a moan she tunneled her fingers through his hair and pressed her body against his.

As she abandoned herself to his kiss, she threw away all doubt about his integrity and his permanent place in her heart. There would never be another man in the world for her. From that first tender embrace long ago to the fiery wonder of Mike in her arms today, there had been a sense of recognition, a sense of coming home each time he held her, as if she'd always known the way he'd taste, the way he'd feel, the way he'd move.

And so it was as they tumbled to the bed. After impatiently ridding himself of his clothes, all except the jaguar tooth necklace, he undressed her with trembling hands. When he faltered she helped, until at last there were no barriers between them.

She touched the smooth jaguar tooth that dangled close to her breasts as he leaned over her.

"Do you want that off, too?"

"No." She used the necklace to pull him closer. "It reminds me of that wild streak in you."

His lips hovered over hers. "Which you've always hated."

"I don't hate it," she whispered, flicking her tongue against his mouth. "I envy it. Show me your wildness, Mike."

"As if I could stop myself, with you here beneath me at last." He closed the tiny gap between them with a searing kiss that was only the beginning of his relentless assault on her senses.

Yet his heated touch on her skin was remembered, somehow. When his mouth captured an aching nipple he generated a liquid warmth that she already knew, and when his breathing quickened, it was a pattern she recognized...her own.

She felt no hesitation, no awkwardness. He knew her, knew the sensual secrets that would arouse her to a greater pitch of excitement. And he, breathing as she breathed, was carried along in the tide of passion. As he knelt between her thighs, she lay before him, unashamed, and his supplicant hands knew the way—his fingers how to knead and lift her breasts to his waiting mouth, his palms how to glide over the curve of her waist as he tasted her.

His mouth traced a path down the valley between her ribs as he slid his hands beneath her. Her breathing changed again, becoming more ragged, for she knew the gift he intended to give her before he plunged deep inside.

She gasped when his tongue probed her sensitive cleft and laved the tender nub awaiting his touch. He raised the stakes, using his tongue to drive her deeper into madness, and a red haze of need swirled through her brain, blotting out everything but her increasingly desperate cries and the pounding urgency at her core.

The mounting tension shivered through her body, setting off responding shudders within him. She clutched his shoulders and quivered, until at last she arched upward in an abandoned, glorious climax, crying out his name again and again.

All boundaries disappeared as she slid both hands down his back to grasp his hips. "I want to feel you deep inside me," she murmured.

"I've always been there."

And so he had. And so he would always be. For she loved only him. "Then come back to me once more," she said.

He sheathed himself. Then, keeping his gaze locked with hers, he entered her, moving smoothly forward, going deep, going for her soul...

She needed to know she'd touched his, as well. "Tell me...it's never been like this."

"Never." He eased back and moved forward again. "And it's never been like this for you."

"That's not a question."

"No." He moved within her, slowly at first, then with increasing speed. "It's not a question."

Her voice became breathy. "You always were a know-it-all, Mike Tremayne."

"I know you." The sweet tension was gradually driving her out of her mind. He shifted his angle slightly, bringing more pressure on that special point he'd awakened not long ago.

"You think...so." Her breath hitched as he made contact with the exact spot. "Well, you're...right." She closed her eyes. "Oh...so...right."

"Open your eyes, Beth. This time I want to watch your eyes while I drive you crazy."

Her eyes drifted open and she looked into his fiery gaze as her body moved in concert with his. Her lips parted and she began to gasp and cry out soft, indistinct words that sounded almost like a plea.

As the moment neared, she began to tremble.

"Yes, my love," he whispered hoarsely. "Explode for me. Shatter into a million pieces. I'll be right here."

"Oh, Mike," she whispered, panting. "Mike...Mike...Mike!" She lifted beneath him.

With an agonized cry of release he plunged with her into the abyss. As he quivered in the aftershock, Beth wrapped her arms around him and drew him down, cradling his head against her shoulder as he lay helpless and dazed.

"I need you so much," he whispered.

She tightened her hold, her eyes damp. She could feel the imprint of the jaguar tooth against her skin, and for now, she'd captured the wildness within him and made it her own. He might never need her like this again, but at least she had this moment when he was completely, utterly hers. No matter what happened, no matter what this moment cost her, it would have to be enough.

9

WAKING UP in unfamiliar surroundings confused Beth at first. She wasn't used to sleeping anywhere except in her apartment above the studio. She turned her head and glanced at the digital bedside clock. Two-ten in the afternoon. She never slept at this time of day. Then she brushed against the man lying next to her, and everything came flooding back. Oh God. She closed her eyes in dismay at the realization that she'd done the one thing she'd sworn never to do. She'd made love to Mike Tremayne.

"Regrets?" murmured a husky voice next to her.

She didn't open her eyes. "How will I ever face Alana?"

"I don't know, seeing as how you can't even face me."

Cautiously she opened her eyes and turned her head on the pillow.

Mike lay watching her, his expression unreadable.

"What have we done?" she whispered.

"You tell me."

"I've betrayed my sister. I've made love to the man she loved. I don't know if she'll ever forgive me."

"In the first place, being true to yourself isn't betraying anyone. And in the second place, whatever Alana's reaction, I was hoping what happened between us would be worth it."

His reminder brought back the delicious memories of

touching and being touched by Mike. She remembered the tender moments they'd shared at the hospital and her decision to make love to this vulnerable man. When he'd stirred her anger, he'd obliterated it again in a blaze of passion. Desire began to push aside her guilt about Alana, as it had a few hours ago.

Mike's expression softened. "That's better. When you get that look in your eyes I know everything will be okay." He raised up so he could see the clock. "I'm going to call the hospital." He swung his legs out of bed. "Just as soon as I find my wallet with the phone number in it, that is."

"It's right here." Beth propped herself on one elbow and reached for the wallet that he'd tossed on the bedside table after taking the condom out.

"Would you get the number for me?" He picked up the receiver of the phone next to him. "It's tucked in behind the bills."

Beth opened the wallet and found the slip of paper. As she passed it across to him she noticed a name scribbled on it. She didn't have much time to read the name, but it looked like Cindy. Cindy had been their waitress at Café Roca two nights ago. She rejected the thought that flashed immediately into her mind—Cindy was a backup in case she hadn't worked out. But the woman in her still had to have her curiosity satisfied. She'd ask him about Cindy later.

As she lay listening to him talk to the nurse on duty, his quiet tone of voice didn't change, so apparently Ernie's condition remained stable. Thank God for that.

"Oh, did she?" Mike said, becoming more alert. He paused. "Yes, I'm glad you filled her in."

A chill passed through Beth as she realized Alana

must have called the hospital. It made sense that she'd do that if she got no answer at Beth's apartment.

"I see," Mike said. "Okay, we'll take our time, then. Thanks for the information." He hung up and turned back to Beth. "Dad's condition has been upgraded and keeps improving."

"I'm glad."

"They're going to be doing some tests for the next couple of hours, so we might as well wait before we go in. We couldn't see him, anyway."

"Okay."

"And Alana called the hospital."

She let out a breath. "I thought so from what you said on the phone."

"She happened to call when one of Dad's doctors was around." His gaze searched hers. "And I guess the doctor filled her in but told her not to worry, that Ernie's son was here taking care of things."

Beth met his gaze. "I see."

"Yeah."

"That's not all the news. I can tell."

He gave her a crooked smile. "It's spooky being around somebody who can read me that well. I've gone years without people being able to do that."

"Habit."

"It's kind of nice, in a weird sort of way," he said.

"You're stalling. What's the rest of the news?"

He ran a hand over the stubble on his chin. "Alana left us a message. She's cutting her trip short and coming home."

Beth absorbed the information but felt no surprise. "I told you she would."

"It might be Ernie's condition bringing her back instead of me."

"I'm sure the doctor told her Ernie's doing just fine and the worst is over. No, it's because you're here, Mike. She's coming back to see you."

"Could be," he admitted.

"So now it starts."

"Not immediately." He stretched out beside her again. "She can't just abandon that family in the Ozarks. It'll take at least twenty-four hours, in my estimation."

"We'll have to tell her about us, won't we?"

He traced the line of her lower lip with one finger. "Of course we will."

"I don't know what I'll say to her."

"Don't think you'll be out there all by yourself." He moved closer and touched his lips to hers. "I'll be there to help."

"We can't make it seem like two against one. That's no fair."

Mike chuckled. "If that isn't a remark straight out of our childhood, I don't know what is."

"I've been thinking about my childhood a lot recently, Mike. Alana always took care of me and made sure I didn't get hurt. Now I'm the one who's hurting her. She doesn't deserve it."

He drew back to study her. "And what do we deserve?"

"I'm not sure."

"Picture this." He slipped an arm around her waist and drew her closer. "An aggressive little girl meets a little boy and immediately decides that he's the one for her."

As she nestled against him and took comfort from his solid length, her anxiety eased. "I know this story."

"Humor me and pay attention, anyway. As she grows up, this girl conditions everybody, including the boy, to think this partnership is their destiny. Her little sister idolizes her, so no problem there. And the boy is flattered that somebody so popular and attractive has picked him out. Sometimes he thinks he likes the little sister better, but saying so would cause a lot of problems, and everything is so damned nice the way it is.''

"You make Alana sound like some sort of tyrant.''

"I don't mean to. I did have a crush on her for a while, and I didn't question myself about whether or not that crush had developed into something that would last a lifetime. Hell, I couldn't imagine myself bucking the lot of you, anyway—Ernie, Pete and my sweet little Beth.'' He caressed her bare bottom. "And you're sweeter than I ever knew.''

"Believe me, I don't feel very sweet right now.''

"Oh, yes, you do.'' He slid a hand up her rib cage and cradled the weight of her breast. "Sugar and spice and everything nice.''

She grew damp and warm as his thumb brushed her nipple. "You'd better stop that. Unless you're more prepared than I thought, we're out of birth control.''

He continued to caress her. "Sad but true. There was but one lonely condom in my wallet.''

Although her thinking was growing fuzzy, she was still alert enough to remember that his wallet had also contained the slip of paper she'd seen a few minutes ago. "And why are you carrying Cindy's name in your wallet, by the way?''

He grinned at her. "Jealous, sweet Beth?''

"Of course not. She's a child. I just—''

"Not such a child.'' As he leaned down and flicked his tongue across her nipple, the jaguar tooth tickled her breast. "Nearly the same age you were when I first kissed you.''

"I was a child then."

"The hell you were." He swirled his tongue over the sensitive areola.

She shuddered in reaction. "I was clueless."

"Then your instincts were incredible. When I kissed you, you rubbed your hips against me until I was hard as a rock."

She pushed him away. "Did not!"

"Did, too." He laughed as he drew her back toward him. "I was ready to throw you down on the grass that minute, but then Dad called from the back door, and that was the end of that. After you went inside, I had to hide out in the bushes for five minutes before my erection disappeared. And don't pretend you didn't know. You must have felt it through that thin silk."

Heat climbed into her cheeks.

"Aha. Just as I thought. You knew exactly how you were affecting me. You and that sexy little red dress. Clueless, my ass."

"I still have that dress."

"Yeah?" He kneaded his way up her backbone. "I suppose you've worn it a lot since then."

"Nope. Never wore it again."

He brushed her hair back from her face. "Wear it for me tonight."

She hadn't thought past the moment. "Tonight?"

"Let me slide that dress from your shoulders, the way I've been dreaming of for eight years." He feathered kisses over her cheeks. "I want to see it fall to the floor, and watch you step out of it. Then I want to make love to you all night."

She closed her eyes as desire took hold of her. "I don't know if we dare. Alana—"

"Alana won't be home that soon, but we'll spend the night at my house, just in case. Give me this, Beth."

She opened her eyes and gazed at him. "All right. We'll at least have that."

"Thank you," he murmured, kissing her. "Oh, and one more thing," he whispered against her mouth, "I want that piece of stained glass."

"It's not for sale."

He outlined her lips with his tongue. "Then I guess you'll have to give it to me."

She snuggled closer and felt the press of his erection against her belly. "You don't want it. You can't cart it through the jungle with you."

"That would be my problem." He took her hand and guided it down to rest on his hardened shaft. "But I want it. You made it for me, and I want it."

She closed her fingers around him. "I didn't make it for you."

"Yes, you did." He moaned softly as she stroked him. "You wanted to tell me..."

"Tell you what?" she asked, her voice seductively low.

"This." He covered her mouth with his and reached down between her thighs.

As his fingers probed her moist sheath, the spring only he could release began to tighten again. She matched his rhythm, massaging him until he began to tremble and groan against her mouth.

He lifted his lips from hers. "Ah, Beth. How I want you."

"You have me."

"I want more. I want to bury myself inside you and say to hell with condoms."

"No, Mike." She gasped as he pushed in deeper. "You don't want to be...tied down."

"Maybe it's all I've ever wanted." His breathing grew ragged.

"I won't let you..." She lost the rest of what she might have said as the tremors took her.

"We've wasted...so much!" With an exasperated cry, he erupted in a warm cascade that spilled over her fingers.

BETH AND MIKE returned to the hospital in the late afternoon. Mike insisted they stop for some fast food and eat it on the way. As they walked down the corridor to Ernie's room, Beth looked down at the rumpled clothes she'd been forced to put on after her shower in the hotel room. "Ugh."

Mike smiled at her concern with appearances when all he had to do was glance at her to become aroused again. He pulled her close and whispered in her ear. "You're beautiful."

"Oh, sure."

He pulled them both to a halt and turned her toward him. "The most beautiful woman I've ever known."

She searched his expression, and her doubtful look indicated she was having a hard time swallowing that statement.

"I suppose you think I'm feeding you a typical meaningless seduction line," he said.

"Under certain circumstances it could qualify."

He glanced around at the hospital atmosphere that surrounded them. "I don't think these are exactly the circumstances." He released her and sighed in exasperation. "Your lack of trust is getting to me, especially because I don't think I've done anything to earn it. Can you give me a single instance when I've lied to you?"

"Other than telling me there were crocodiles in the drainage ditches?"

"That was make-believe and you knew it. I mean about serious stuff."

"I hope you haven't, Mike."

He lifted his eyebrows. "Meaning?"

"I'm choosing to believe your story over Alana's. If I ever find out that it's not true—"

"It's true, even though I understand why you wouldn't want to believe it."

"On the contrary. Believing you is the only way I can live with myself. So you'd better be telling me the truth."

"I am. Now let's go see how that ornery old guy is doing." He took her hand as they continued down toward Ernie's room. So she trusted him for now, he thought as he walked beside her down the hallway. He wondered if she would still trust him when Alana came home and called him a liar. Because unless Alana had changed, that's exactly what she'd do.

Mike braced himself to see a sicker-looking version of his father as they walked into his room. Fortunately Ernie was awake with his bed rolled partway up. Although his color still wasn't great, he didn't look nearly as pale as he had the night before.

He managed a smile. "Well, look who's here. You two decide to knock off work and drive up together?"

Mike realized his father might not remember they'd both been there the night before. "Something like that," he said. "You gave us a scare, Dad."

"So they tell me." His attention turned to Beth. "You're shinin' like a new penny. Suits you."

Mike glanced at Beth to see how she was taking that.

Sure enough, she was blushing. "I'm just happy you came through this thing okay," she said.

"That's flatterin' but I don't think an old geezer like me is what put such a bloom on you."

Her blush deepened. "I—"

"Never mind. Come give me a peck on the cheek and then let me talk to Mike alone for a bit."

Beth followed Ernie's instructions. "Get better," she said as she kissed him. Then she walked past Mike on her way out of the room. Her glance told him clearly that she didn't want him giving Ernie any details of their recent encounter.

He shook his head slightly to let her know he wouldn't.

"I'll just be down the hall, schmoozing with the nurses," she said as she left the room.

"Come here, Mike," Ernie said when she was gone.

Mike felt almost like a kid again as he responded to his father's summons. He pulled up a chair next to the bed and sat down. "I'm here, Dad."

"Something's happenin' between you two, isn't it?"

"Yeah."

"Serious?"

"Yeah."

"Alana's comin' home."

Mike nodded. "I know."

"I wanna know if you're gonna be able to handle this."

Mike gazed into his father's eyes, dark with unexpressed physical pain. "I'll handle it, Dad. I screwed it up eight years ago, but I'll handle it this time."

"Good." His father closed his eyes.

Mike touched Ernie's arm. His skin was alarmingly dry and papery. "Want me to call the nurse?"

"No. I'm okay." Ernie opened his eyes. "Damned nuisance. I need to be there in case things go bad."

"I won't let them go bad."

"Pete said he might be able to be there, but I don't know if he can."

Mike started to panic. His father was hallucinating. "Let me get a nurse, Dad."

His eyes flew open. "No!" Then a faint smile touched his lips. "Oh, I see what you're worried about. That business about Pete wanting to be there."

"Pete's gone, Dad."

"Not quite, he ain't."

"Dad—"

"Listen, Mike. I'm gonna tell you this, but you gotta promise you won't tell none of the people in this hospital."

"Dad, I can't promise that. Too much is at stake, here."

"Then I ain't telling you."

Mike glared at him and soon decided it was better that somebody hear this confession, whatever it was. "Okay, I promise."

"First of all, I ain't crazy. Second of all, when I had the heart attack, I met Pete on the other side. Since then he's been talkin' to me."

"Dad," Mike said gently, "certain drugs can make you think that—"

"It ain't the drugs. But never mind. The point I wanna make is that Pete and me always knew you and Beth should be together. See, Alana needs lots of people around her, but you and Beth, you're more the solitary type. Your personalities just fit, y'know? So Pete and me, we're pulling for you two to work it out."

"Oh, boy." Mike slumped back in the chair and stared

at the ceiling. First his father admitted he was talking to the dead, and now he claimed to have known all along what Mike was just finding out. "How come you never said that you thought Beth was the one for me instead of Alana?"

"Ha. I hope you have a kid someday and he's a know-it-all just like you. Back then I couldn't tell you the sky was blue, let alone you'd picked the wrong Nightingale girl. But maybe you've growed up enough to fix it. Beth's the one you need to marry."

Mike sat forward in the chair again. "Wait a minute, Dad. I never said a thing about marrying Beth. Sure, we get along great, but I don't know if I'm cut out for marriage. And Beth wants to stay in Bisbee, don't forget. I'm not planning to give up my trips to South America, so I don't know if—"

"Yammer, yammer, yammer. You should listen to yourself. When you love a woman, you make adjustments. She makes adjustments. Life's too short not to."

When you love a woman. His father was forcing him to acknowledge what he'd been unwilling to admit to himself, even after all the years of fantasizing, even after the glory of what he'd shared with Beth only hours ago. He'd been unwilling to admit to an emotion so strong because then his life would truly change forever.

"Cat got your tongue?" his father asked, his voice faint.

Mike realized his father had closed his eyes again and was looking very tired. "I was just thinking about what you said," he said. "Listen, I should go so you can get some rest."

"I could use a nap, I guess."

"Then you do that." Mike stood. As he leaned down to press his lips against his father's forehead, the jaguar tooth necklace shifted beneath his shirt. He straightened and pulled the leather cord over his head. "I need you to hang onto this for me, Dad," he said. He half expected an argument as he lifted his father's head from the pillow and slipped on the necklace.

Ernie just looked at him. "I can see you're bound I should have this thing around my neck."

"Humor me."

"Guess I hafta. Judy'll get a real charge out of this here tooth."

"Everything's gonna be okay, Dad."

"You bet."

Mike swallowed. "See you soon, Dad."

10

CLOUDS BUBBLED like giant soapsuds on the horizon as Mike and Beth headed toward the Time Tunnel in the Mule Mountains. At six in the evening the sun still baked the Arizona desert, and the rental car's air-conditioning was turned up to high.

Beth took off her sunglasses as they entered the tunnel. The closer they got to Bisbee, the more she sensed impending disaster. "She'll be here soon, Mike. I can feel it."

"So she'll be here." He laid his sunglasses on the dash and reached for her hand. "I want you to know that I'm not going to confront her about the lie. I understand why she did it, and as long as you believe my version, I'm willing to let it go. Maybe she wants to let it go, too."

"That's possible, but I'll bet she'll try to start things up again with you."

"Not if we let her know right away that we're involved."

She took a deep breath. "God, that's going to be hard."

"We can do it together."

"No, I think I should tell her by myself."

He squeezed her hand. "So it won't be two against one?"

"Something like that." As the car emerged from the

tunnel, Beth tried to convince herself that Alana would be able to handle the news. It was a tough sell.

"This has put us another day behind on the cutters," Mike said.

"I can live with that. All things considered, the cutter schedule doesn't seem very important right now."

Mike made the left-hand turn into town and headed toward the glass studio. The mountains surrounding the town threw Main Street into shadow, which gave an illusion of coolness to the evening. "The cutter schedule might be more important than you realize."

"What do you mean?"

"If sales start going through the roof, you'd have the capital to expand into other countries."

"Other countries?" She laughed in disbelief. "Oh, right, Mike. Like where, Brazil?"

"Why not? Instead of desert scenes, you could make rain forest windows. Think of what a scarlet macaw would look like in stained glass."

The concept appealed to her immediately. "Or think of orchids, or a toucan, or even a yellow-and-black jaguar with green eyes." Her glance went instinctively to the spot where the leather necklace made a slight imprint under his shirt. It wasn't there. "Mike, your necklace. Don't tell me you've lost—"

"No. I gave it to my dad."

"Oh." She was afraid the gesture meant he was more concerned about his father than he'd let on. "For good luck?"

"In a way." His gaze met hers for a moment. "Hey, don't look so worried. He needed a conversation starter, that's all. Something to amuse the nurses until he gets his rubber cigar back."

"Okay." She wasn't convinced, but she wouldn't push the issue.

"Anyway, back to your proposed expansion." He pulled up in front of the studio and stopped the car, but left the engine running. "If you'd even consider Brazil, you might want to make a trip down there sometime. I could take you. We could investigate the idea of a satellite studio."

She stared at him, her heart pounding. "What are you saying?"

He turned to look at her. "I don't know yet," he said softly. "Just thinking out loud a little. How does any of that strike you?"

"You wouldn't be happy helping me run a satellite glass studio in Brazil."

"You always seem so sure that you know what would and wouldn't make me happy."

"Mike, I know you! You've always wanted to explore the jungle. As soon as you left Bisbee you headed straight for the Amazon, and before long there you were, guiding expeditions through the most remote corners of the rain forest."

"You never asked if I've been happy doing that."

"Okay, have you?"

"Sometimes. Sometimes I feel like the loneliest guy in the universe. Ever since I left here there's been a big chunk missing out of my life, Beth. I never wanted to admit what it was." He paused and studied her. "Or who I was missing."

She struggled not to become giddy with hope. She had to remember what he'd been through in the past few days, and how the stress might have affected his emotions. Once Ernie was well, he might revert to his former independent self. "I'm afraid you'd get impatient, taking an inexperienced person like me into your beloved rain forest."

"Are you kidding? I'd love showing it to you. Both you and my dad, as a matter of fact. I know you wouldn't want to go as deep into the jungle as I've gone, but—"

"Don't be so sure."

He regarded her quietly for a moment. "It seems we've both been making assumptions."

"Yes, it does."

He took a deep breath and let it out. "Wow. It's been quite a day."

"I'd say so."

"And it's not over yet." He touched the tip of his finger to her nose. "So you'd better go upstairs and find that red dress. I'll be back in an hour to pick you up. I— oh, hell." His attention moved beyond her. "Here comes Huxford."

She turned in the seat, and sure enough, Colby was approaching the car. She unsnapped her seat belt. "I'll take care of him."

Mike turned off the engine. "No, I'll take care of him. The guy is invading my space, and I don't like it."

"Mike, I think it would be better if I handled this."

"Afraid I'll tick him off?"

"Yes, frankly."

"What difference does it make? His company's not getting the patent, and he's not getting you, so he can take a flying leap, as far as I'm concerned. I think I'll just tell him so." He opened the door.

"Mike! I'm asking you not to confront him! I'll fight my own battles!"

He closed the door again and turned to gaze at her. "Or could it be that you don't want to fight at all? Could it be that you want to keep Huxford hanging around, as a backup?"

"That's unfair! And speaking of backups, you never did explain why you had Cindy's name on that piece of paper!"

"So I could remember to tell my dad hello for her. Which I forgot to do, in all the excitement. She really likes Ernie and wants him to get better."

"Oh."

"Huxford's waiting for you on the sidewalk. Better go talk to him."

She picked up her purse. "Mike, he's not a backup."

His glance was intense. "No, he's not." In a quick move he pulled her toward him and kissed her so thoroughly that she dropped her purse. Finally, when they were both breathing hard, he released her. "And now he knows it," he said in a voice husky with desire.

She straightened her blouse and steadied her breathing. "Was that absolutely necessary?"

"Yep. See you in an hour. We'll eat at the Copper Queen. Wear your red dress."

"I just might wear blue." She picked up her purse again and opened the car door.

"Bet you don't."

She closed the car door without comment, and Mike drove away, leaving her to face Colby alone. But that was what she'd asked for. She hadn't asked him to kiss her so possessively in front of Colby, however.

"I was worried about you," Colby said as he came toward her. "People around here said you never close your shop on a weekday unless there's some sort of emergency."

"There was. Mike's father had another medical crisis."

"So you were comforting him just now?"

She wished she'd left her sunglasses on. "Colby, I'd like to keep my personal business out of our discussions, if you don't mind."

"You're about to make a fool of yourself, you know."

"Colby, please. If you'll excuse me, I've had a long day and I need to go inside and check my messages." She took her keys from her purse and started toward the shop.

He followed her. "You're throwing away the opportunity of a lifetime because of some guy who'll leave you high and dry."

She turned back to him. "What am I throwing away? I thought you agreed I could have a two-week extension before signing the contract."

"I wasn't talking about the damned contract!"

She looked at him without comprehending. When she finally did, she had a most inappropriate reaction. She laughed.

"Oh, so you think it's funny?" His face contorted with anger. "You think a personal liaison with me is so ridiculous that it makes you laugh?"

She sobered immediately. "I'm sorry, Colby. That was really awful of me. I didn't mean to insult you. It's just that I've had quite a time of it, and not much sleep. I'm worried about Mike's father, and sometimes nervous anxiety makes people laugh at the wrong times. I've even heard of people laughing at funerals."

"An appropriate comparison. This will be the funeral of your precious cutter promotion, I can assure you."

So he was withdrawing his company's offer. She felt relieved. "I'm sorry you feel that way, but I understand. I'm sure Handmade can survive just fine without this tool in their inventory."

"Oh, I expect to get your cutter patent for Handmade eventually. I expect you'll soon be begging me to give you something, *anything* for the patent. But we didn't have to play hardball, you and I. I had hoped this could be a mutually satisfying experience." His gaze raked over her. "On several levels. But it's obvious from what I saw in the car and the whisker burn on your face that Tremayne got there ahead of me."

She hadn't realized she was going to slap him until her palm connected with his face. She'd forgotten she still held her keys in that same hand. The edge of her door key bit into his cheek, and as they stood staring at each other in shock, he began to bleed.

"Oh, dear," she said, reaching toward him. "I didn't mean—"

"Keep away from me," he snarled, backing up. "You've made your choice. Now we'll see if you can live with it."

"Colby, I apologize. Really, the tension has been terrific recently. I really didn't intend to hurt you like that. I forgot the keys were still in my hand."

"As they used to say in the Old West, it's only a scratch." He continued to back away down the sidewalk. "You'll be the one who'll bleed in the end, Beth. I could have prevented that, but there's no stopping it now."

She gazed after him, not sure why he felt he could make such dire predictions. Mike would return to the cutter manufacturing tomorrow, and she felt confident he'd keep the orders filled until other machinists were trained to take over the operation. Eventually Ernie would return to supervise, and then...then maybe some of those expansion plans Mike had talked about could be considered. She still couldn't picture Mike putting those plans into operation personally, but that didn't mean it wasn't a good idea, or that she and Mike couldn't devise a way to see each other more often. From her perspective the future of the Nightingale-Tremayne partnership, both business and personal, looked bright.

Still puzzled by Colby's behavior, she unlocked the shop and walked inside to turn off the security system. Apparently Colby was just a sore loser who thought she'd be frightened by such talk. He didn't understand the new confidence she had now that Mike was in her corner.

She walked behind the counter and punched the Play button on her answering machine.

The first message was Alana's, a cheerful *"Greetings from deep in the Ozarks."* Alana paused, obviously waiting for Beth to pick up the phone. *"Guess you're in the shower or something,"* she said, sounding disappointed. *"I'll call back."*

Beth's stomach knotted. When she was with Mike, she could push aside the sense of betrayal she felt concerning Alana, but her sister's upbeat voice on the answering machine brought her guilt back full force. Mike might want to believe that Alana wasn't still in love with him, but Beth knew better.

The next message was also Alana's. *"Beth? You around yet?"* Another pause. *"Guess not. Maybe we got our signals crossed and you forgot I was supposed to call today. I'd really like an update on Ernie, though. I had a dream about Ernie and Dad last night, and it made me—I don't know—really homesick, I guess you could say. Maybe I'll just call the hospital in a little while and check on him."*

Beth gazed out the front window of the shop. Enough light remained in the day to filter through the vivid colors of *The Embrace.* She'd always thought Alana hadn't known who the piece represented. What if she'd been wrong, and the work had been taunting Alana with the past all along?

The next three messages were business calls, followed by a message from Colby.

Then Alana came on again. *"So Mike's back. Listen, all this stuff with Ernie is scaring the bejeezus out of me, Bethy. I've met some people around here, and there's a rafting company that will probably finish up the trip with my family for a reasonable price. Assuming I can arrange that, I'm flying home. It'll probably be standby, so don't worry about when I'll get there. Hope you've been getting along okay with Mike. He may be a rascal, but after all, we have a lot of history together, the three of us. Maybe it's time to bury the hatchet. See you soon."*

Beth forced herself to make notes on the rest of the messages from customers, although all she could hear was Alana's voice, and the barely disguised eagerness to see Mike again. It would have been bad enough for Alana to come home and discover Mike wasn't at all interested in her. But to come home and find out he was involved with Beth, instead—that might be more than Alana could take. In all their years together Beth had never crossed her older sister, because crossing her might mean Alana would withdraw her love. Nothing had ever been worth taking that risk—until now.

THE RED DRESS FIT a little more snugly in the bodice and hips than it had eight years ago. Worried that it was too form-fitting, Beth changed out of it twice, but Mike arrived at the back door just as she'd put it on again. She ran down the stairs to answer the door.

He stood there holding a bouquet of flowers she recognized as coming from Ernie's cherished rose garden.

His eyes widened and his lips parted as he gazed at her without speaking.

"I know it's too tight," she said, smoothing the skirt. "Give me a minute and I'll change into something else."

"Don't you dare."

"Mike, I like to wear my clothes much looser. Something this snug feels too provocative."

He stepped inside and laid the flowers on a table near the back door. "Can you imagine how I'd feel if you set out to be provocative, just for me?" He took her by the shoulders and gazed down at her. "I'd feel like a king, Beth."

"I...never thought of it that way."

"No, I'll bet you haven't. You've made a career out of blending into the background, which is why it took me so long to figure out how much I wanted you."

He was right, she realized. She'd always tried to avoid competing with Alana for attention, knowing instinctively that Alana wouldn't like that. Once in her life she'd bought a dress that demanded attention—this dress—and the results had been catastrophic.

He caressed her bare arms. "Do you remember how I teased you about the way you ate your ice cream, and you said it was unintentional?"

"Well, it was!"

"Next time you do something sexy like that, make it intentional."

She looked into his eyes and excitement settled deep within her. "I might not know how to be like that."

"A creative woman like you? You know how."

Perhaps she did, she thought, as her anticipation of flirting with him grew. "Wait here," she said. "I'll go put the flowers in water."

"I'll go with you."

"No." She smiled at him. "Wait here." She picked up the bouquet and buried her nose in it. "These are wonderful. Thank you." Then she turned and started up the stairs. Her natural inclination would have been to skip up the steps and get the job done quickly, but Mike had given her a few ideas. She mounted the steps slowly, moving her hips in invitation as she climbed.

Halfway up she turned and glanced down at him. "How's that?"

His reply was thick with desire. "It's taking all my willpower not to follow you up those stairs and ravish you on the landing."

"Then I guess I'm getting the idea."

"I never doubted you would."

She continued up the stairs, a wide grin on her face. The red dress still felt tight, but she was no longer upset by it.

MIKE SAT ACROSS FROM BETH at a linen-draped table on the balcony of the Copper Queen Hotel as they waited for the dinner they'd ordered to arrive. Candlelight from a votive on the table caressed her face and flashed in the simple gold chain she wore around her neck. She absorbed his attention completely. The red silk emphasized the swell of her breasts and exposed just enough cleavage to make his mouth water. She'd arranged her hair in a more complicated way than it had been fixed eight years ago, but that was okay. He was glad they were both eight years older, eight years wiser. That made everything that happened between them all the richer.

As they'd walked hand in hand from her studio to the historic Copper Queen, men had gazed after her in admiration. Mike had watched her gain confidence from the admiring stares and knew he'd take a more aggressive woman to bed with him tonight. The thought made him long to forgo dinner altogether.

But he wanted this to be a night they'd remember for the rest of their lives, and having dinner together was part of the fantasy that would end in glorious lovemaking. The first time had been borne of crisis and muddled with issues that had to be settled before they could fully love each other. Tonight he wanted magic.

But he decided they had to get a couple of topics discussed and out of the way first. "I called the hospital just before I walked down to your studio. Dad's progress is still good."

"I know. I called, too," Beth admitted. "The staff must get sick of all these calls, but I had to make sure nothing more had happened since we left this afternoon."

"After that scare last night, I'm not taking anything for granted. I figured we could drive back up there after work tomorrow."

"I'd like that." A shadow crossed her expression. "Of course, I don't think it will be just the two of us by then."

That was the second topic, he thought. "Okay, tell me what message she left on your machine. Then I think we should ban that discussion for the rest of the night."

"She said that Ernie's condition was scaring her, and that she'd try to arrange for a local rafting company to finish guiding the family through their trip so she can fly home. She thinks it's time we all buried the hatchet."

"That sounds innocent enough."

"On the surface." Beth sipped from her water goblet. "But her tone was so eager, Mike. I could tell the way she said it that she can hardly wait to see you, and I know she'll build a whole scenario around the two of you finally realizing you're meant for each other."

He reached across the table and laced his fingers through hers. He'd been dying to touch her ever since they sat down. "Right scenario, wrong woman."

She glanced down at their interlaced fingers. "Every time I think about her reaction, I get chills."

"That's why we're not going to think about it any more tonight. There's no way this can turn out the way Alana wants." He hesitated, but knew he had to say it. "Of course, you still have the option of telling me to get lost. I won't say anything to Alana, and neither will Ernie, if I ask him not to."

Beth glanced up with a faint smile. "Ready to make a noble gesture again?"

"Hell, no. But as I've said before, I want this to be a decision you can live with. And I won't pretend the next few days will be easy on any of us."

"If I wanted to keep our relationship a secret, I shouldn't have agreed to sit holding hands with you on the balcony of the Copper Queen. Half the town passes by here every night. And there's that little matter of our public kiss two nights ago, and the one in the car this afternoon. I'm sure the word is out." She took a deep breath, which drew his attention to the drape of silk over her breasts. "The die is cast, as they say in dramatic movies. Oh, and speaking of drama, I might as well tell you what happened with Colby Huxford."

He tensed. "What about him?"

"After you left his afternoon, he told me I was throwing away the opportunity of a lifetime. At first I thought he meant with the cutter, but when I realized he meant with *him*, I'm afraid I...laughed."

Mike smiled. "You have no idea what that does for my ego."

"It didn't do much for his. He made some crude remark about you getting there ahead of him, and before I knew it, I'd slapped him. Only I forgot my keys were still in my hand, so the edge of one cut his cheek. It was more damage than I intended to do, to be honest."

"Not half as much as I intend to do if I ever catch that slime-bucket talking to you again."

"I don't think he'll be asking me out anymore, but he was predicting that my plan for the cutter is doomed and he'd get it, after all."

"Well, he's wrong. We missed a day today, but we'll make it up. I also called the guy from Sierra Vista and apologized about not meeting him at the shop this morning like we'd talked about. I offered to pay him anyway, so he's happy. He's coming back tomorrow and bringing a friend, so I expect production will really pick up."

Beth frowned and cleared her throat. "Look, I want to help pay these extra people, Mike. Things are slow for me right now, but soon I'll—"

"Hey," he said softly.

"What?"

"My dad's put me in charge of his shop, to run it as I see fit. The charge to you for the cutters will be the same as it's always been. However, if you want to talk business sometime, I'd like to buy into Nightingale-Tremayne, Inc."

She looked astonished. "You mean invest in our company?"

"That's right." He brought her hand up to his lips. "I like the looks of it. This Nightingale woman seems to know her stuff." He slowly kissed each of her long, slender fingers and thought of what pleasure they would bring him tonight.

"Aren't you automatically part of the company, being Ernie's son?"

"No. Years ago I foolishly told him I didn't want to be listed on any of the partnership papers, so now I'm forced to buy in. Serves me right."

"I wouldn't know what to do with an investor, that's for sure."

He couldn't help grinning as he gazed across the table at her. God, she was beautiful. "I have a few suggestions for what you could do with this one."

11

WHEN MIKE HAD TOLD BETH they were having dinner at the Copper Queen, her first thought had been that she'd prefer somewhere more secluded than the primary watering hole for the entire town. Yet she discovered as the meal continued that she lost all sense of what was going on around her. Except for the occasional person who called out a greeting from the street, or the necessary interruptions of the waiter serving them, she narrowed her focus to Mike, and he'd seemed totally concentrated on her, as well.

For the first time in her life, she flirted outrageously. She slipped her foot from her shoe to rub her stocking foot against his calf and delighted in the way his eyes darkened. She asked for a taste of his meal and held his hand steady while she took the morsel slowly and sensuously from his fork into her mouth. She dipped her finger into the tiny bowl of ranch salad dressing and then licked it off. She made certain he was watching her before she swirled the tip of her tongue over a drop of moisture that was running down the side of her water goblet.

That maneuver brought a muffled groan. "I've created a monster."

"I never realized teasing a man could be so much fun."

"I never realized it could be such torture."

"You asked me to do this. You said it would make you feel like a king."

"I did and it does." He lowered his voice. "The downside is that the family jewels are in severe distress."

She gave him a mischievous grin. "That's a shame. Are we staying for dessert?"

"Not on your life." He signaled for the check.

"Then maybe we should stop for an ice cream cone on the way home."

"Nothing doing," he muttered under his breath. "I'm not giving you a chance to play any more games until we're someplace where I can play, too."

"Are you inviting me to come over to your house to play, Mikey?" she asked with a seductive glance.

"That about sums it up." He tossed some bills on the table next to the check and came around to help her out of her chair. "We'll start with spin the bottle."

"I don't think there will be much challenge in that, with only two of us." She deliberately brushed against him as she moved away from the table.

"Think again." He took firm possession of her arm and guided her back through the indoor section of the restaurant. A couple of diners waved to them and tried to engage Beth in conversation. "Sorry, can't talk right now," Mike said through clenched teeth as he propelled Beth out the door and down the steps of the Copper Queen.

"You certainly are in a hurry," she said as he grabbed her hand and practically tugged her up Main Street. "Don't you think it would be a nice time to window-shop?"

"Nope."

"A nightcap in Brewery Gulch?"

"Nope."

They were walking very fast as they left the commercial section of Main and continued up the road into a residential area where trees arched over the uneven sidewalk. As she skipped along beside him and noticed the grim set of his jaw, she was having a hard time keeping herself from laughing. She'd never seen him in such a mood, and all because of a few well-chosen tactics on her part. "Perhaps you'd like to drag me to your house by my hair."

"Don't tempt me."

"Oh, but that's exactly what you told me to do."

"How did I know you'd be so damned good at it?"

As they left the main road and headed up the side street that led to the Tremayne house, she was breathing hard from the exertion. "Mike, stop a minute. These little red pumps weren't made for cross-country. I have to catch my breath."

He stopped immediately and turned, his expression concerned. "I'm sorry, Beth. I..." His voice trailed off as his gaze traveled to her heaving bosom and he groaned. "Do you have to *breathe* like that?"

"I'm afraid so." But she was gasping a little more dramatically, just for his benefit. "My heart is pounding. Just feel it." She placed his hand against her breast.

He sucked in a breath and pulled her hard against him. "You are out of control," he muttered just before his lips came down on hers.

And so she was. The rustle of the silk dress as he crushed her against him brought back everything about that summer night eight years ago, when she first discovered the woman deep inside her, the woman who wanted to give herself to a man, this man. That woman had seemed to disappear, but perhaps she'd only been hoarding her gifts until they could once again be spread before the only one who could appreciate them. And now he was back.

His mouth moved from her lips to her throat and down to the cleft between her breasts. "God help me, I want to undress you here on the street. I've never thought of doing anything like that in my life."

"Never?" she murmured.

"Okay, once before." He lifted his head and gazed down at her, his expression shadowed. "And it was you that time, too."

"And instead you ran away."

"It would have torn us all apart then."

"And now?"

"I won't let that happen." With an obvious effort he backed away from her and took her hand again. "Come on, before I embarrass us both in the streets of Bisbee."

In a few moments they were inside the familiar surroundings of Mike's house, where Beth had played as a child, where she'd done homework assignments with Mike and Alana, where they'd watched hours of television, shared untold cans of soda and countless bags of chips. And where, ultimately, the celebration had moved after Alana and Mike's wedding rehearsal dinner at the Copper Queen. Ernie had strung the trees surrounding the little Victorian house with hundreds of tiny lights, but there had been one darkened corner of the yard where the lights hadn't reached, and there Mike and Beth had kissed for the very first time.

Mike had left a soft light burning in the kitchen toward the back of the house, but the rest of it, the small living room, the dining nook, the two bedrooms, all of which Beth remembered in perfect detail, were cast in shadow. The air was scented with roses. Beth wondered if the fragrance came from an open window next to Ernie's fabled rose garden.

"Oh, Mike, the memories that are in here," Beth said.

"I know." He took her in his arms. "But they'll be with us forever. We might as well make them a part of loving each other now."

"In your bedroom?"

"That's right."

"On the bed we used to pretend was a dugout going down the Amazon?"

"We can still pretend that." He held her tightly, his body taut and aroused. "I never admitted this to myself, let alone you, but I wanted to take you deep into the jungle with me back then. And remember how we used to wrestle? Even when we were teenagers?"

She moved seductively against him. "I loved wrestling with you," she murmured.

"I know you did. You loved having me touch you, and I loved doing it, but we pretended to ourselves it was just fooling around."

"Because we had to pretend that."

"We don't have to pretend anymore." His kiss teased her mouth open and his tongue set up a lazy rhythm that soon had quickened her breathing and weakened her knees. Gently he released her. "Stay here a minute. I'll be right back for you."

She stood in the darkened living room surrounded by the old familiar furniture Ernie had never replaced. In the dim light she couldn't see how worn the cushions had become, or the stains from all the snacks eaten there. She waited for her conscience to chastise her for shamelessly agreeing to spend the night making love to Mike in this house. Instead she felt only a warm certainty that she was where she belonged.

Mike returned and led her into the bedroom where she'd spent so many make-believe hours as a child. She stepped forward into a different sort of fantasy world. The tropical mural still took up one wall, but tonight the flickering candles set on every available surface gave the jungle panorama a dark, mysterious cast. The muted rhythms of a drum and flute created a sensuous tribal beat, and the covers on the bed were turned back to reveal snowy sheets...strewn with rose petals. So that had been the reason for the sweet scent.

Standing close behind her, he pulled her back toward him and nuzzled her ear. "I wanted orchids, but roses will have to do."

"Roses are wonderful." She surveyed his handiwork once again. The magical scene appealed to the sensual nature that had made her an artist. With her newfound courage, she decided to embellish this fantasy he'd begun. When he started to unzip her dress, she stepped away from him and held up her hand. "Not yet."

His voice was thick with desire. "I want you, Beth."

"And soon you'll want me even more." She took the pins from her hair and dropped them to the floor. Her hair tumbled around her shoulders. "I love your crazy sense of adventure," she murmured. "I always have." Then she reached behind her back and slowly drew down the zipper of her dress. "You're impulsive. That excites me."

"Underneath, you're just as wild as I am."

"You're the only one who seems to have figured that out." She allowed the red dress to slide from her shoulders. The fabric was light and it took a long time to slip over her breasts to her waist, and over her hips. Finally she stood in a scarlet pool of silk, revealing bits of red lace and silk that barely covered her, and a red garter belt. "I took pains to make sure nobody knew how I craved excitement."

Mike didn't move a muscle as she unveiled her secrets, but his breathing grew more labored.

"But my wild streak needed an outlet," she continued. "I bought all this to go with the dress."

His voice sounded strained. "That's what you had on underneath your dress that night?"

"Yes." She slid both hands up her ribs and over her breasts.

His hungry gaze followed.

"And it made me bold for the first time in my life," she continued. "I got what I'd always secretly wanted, too. I saw you watching me all night, and when we walked into the shadows, I knew what would happen."

"If Ernie hadn't called to us," he said fervently, "I would have found out what you had on under that dress. I went crazy."

"So did I." She unfastened her gold necklace and let it drop to the floor along with the dress. "Some part of me couldn't stand the thought that you were marrying Alana. Some primitive instinct made me want to be seductive that night. I told myself it was your fault and the champagne's fault that we kissed, but that isn't true."

"Thank you for telling me that."

"Ah, but I'll tell you more." She unhooked the front clasp of her bra and shrugged it from her shoulders as he drew in a sharp breath. "After you left town, sometimes I'd pretend that you'd come back and climbed in through my bedroom window." She cradled one breast in her hand and lightly circled the nipple with her finger. "I imagined you were touching me like this."

He made a low, indistinct noise in the back of his throat.

She continued to tease him with the caress. "Did you ever imagine that?"

"Yes."

She released her breast before the stimulation caused her to throw herself into his arms and end the game. As his arousal grew, so did hers. Fine tremors shook her as she leaned down to unhook her stockings. Stepping out of her shoes, she eased each stocking down in turn. When she glanced up at him, his jaw was set and his hands were clenched at his sides. The raging passion in his eyes provided her reward.

She slid the garter belt over her hips and let it fall to the floor. "And sometimes, I'd imagine you were touching me like this." Holding his gaze, she slipped her hand beneath the scrap of silk to the moist channel waiting for him.

He groaned. "Beth..."

"You were my fantasy lover." She shivered as her fingers came in contact with the pulsing center of her passion. As she dared to caress herself while he watched, her heartbeat thundered in her ears, and she knew her control was nearly destroyed. The game must come to a close. Slowly withdrawing her hand, she pushed the panties down and kicked them away.

At last she walked to the bed and lay back on the petal-strewn sheets. The velvet texture of the roses caressed her bare skin, and the scent of crushed petals filled the room as she gazed up at him. "Make my fantasies come true, Mike," she whispered.

Releasing a long-held breath, he pulled away his clothing in rough, jerky movements.

"Easy, my sweet lover," she murmured.

His movements slowed, but not much. Taking a packet from a table beside the bed, he sheathed himself quickly. Yet when he eased onto the bed, he didn't pull her into his arms, as she might have expected from the intensity in his gaze.

Instead he lay propped on his side, not touching her. Scooping up a handful of rose petals, he dribbled them slowly over her breasts and down her body, allowing them to trickle between her thighs.

She quivered as the cool petals drifted over her heated skin.

Picking one from her breast, he used it as if it were a feather. He brushed her mouth, her throat, her nipples, the valley between her breasts, until she began to whimper with unfulfilled need. He continued to caress her, drawing the rose petal over her flat stomach and along the inside of her quivering thighs.

"Please," she begged, twisting in the velvet nest of rose petals. "Please."

He released the petal and moved over her to kneel between her thighs. "In your fantasy you imagined me touching you here," he murmured, capturing her breast and leaning down to take her nipple in his mouth.

"Yes." The firm suction made her gasp and arch upward into his caress. "Oh, yes."

Shifting to her other breast, he pleasured her for long moments, as the tension mounted within her.

At last he lifted his head to gaze down at her. "And here." He slipped his hand between them, pushing aside rose petals as his fingers tunneled through the triangle of curls between her thighs to massage the slick nub that ached for him.

"Yes!" she cried.

He leaned down, and his voice was hoarse as he spoke against her ear. "I almost lost it when you touched yourself like this."

She gasped as he probed deep.

He stroked her relentlessly. "Did it feel this good?"

She could barely speak. "No...never."

"And did you want more?"

Her breath came in short, frenzied pants. "Yes...yes...yes."

"Do you want more now, my wild Beth?"

"Please, Mike. Please!"

He lifted his head and looked into her eyes as he slowly withdrew his fingers and trailed his hand back up the length of her body. Then he rubbed his fingers against her mouth, urging her lips apart. "Can you taste how much you want me?" he murmured.

She ran her tongue over her kiss-swollen lips. "Yes."

"I want you even more than that. Before the night is over you'll taste how much I want you, too."

"Yes." Her heart beat wildly.

"If I could hold back now, I would, because I want you to be driven out of your mind the way you drove me out of mine."

"But you can't hold back, can you?" she whispered.

"No...I can't." With a groan he pushed deep.

She cried out with joy at the completeness of their joining, the ecstasy of being filled by him.

"You belong in the jungle," he crooned against her ear. "You're full of jungle heat."

"You're the source of my heat," she murmured.

"We are the source." He began an insistent rhythm that mimicked the steady beat of the drums as the weight of his chest on hers crushed the rose petals against her breasts. "Someday I'll take you like this on a bed of ferns, deep in the forest, and the wild animals will hear your cries."

"And yours," she said, gasping.

"And mine. Ah, Beth, this is no fantasy." His breath came faster now as the pace increased. "This is...real."

"I know," she cried, just before he propelled her to a shattering climax. A second later he exploded with his own. She held on tight as the world tilted, then gradually righted itself. "I know," she murmured again as the scent of rose petals surrounded them in a riot of fragrance.

ALTHOUGH HE'D HAD LESS than three hours' sleep in the past twenty-four, Mike was determined not to spend this night sleeping, either. He had her now, but he still wasn't confident he'd have her after Alana came home. If Beth had to choose between the sister she'd known and loved all her life and the man who'd only recently come back into her world, the pull of family might make her choose Alana. Every moment he spent loving her would improve his chances, however, so he allowed himself only short catnaps during the night.

Rejecting sleep wasn't that difficult; the need to make love to Beth always woke him after a little while, anyway. Apparently desire ruled her, as well, because he could rouse her with a mere touch. True, it sometimes mattered *where* that touch came as to how effectively he brought her out of sleep, but he grew adept at knowing her sensual trigger points.

As they loved the night away, she delighted him with her imaginative approach. Before long, she was as intimately acquainted with every inch of his body as he was with hers, and just the memory of what she could accomplish with her mouth and tongue was enough to make him ache all over again. Her expertise didn't come from experience, it seemed. Gradually, from obscure comments she'd made, he'd pieced together the information about her love life since he'd been gone, and she'd only been intimate with two men. Neither relationship had lasted very long or consisted of much passion, which gave him a great deal of satisfaction.

Early in the morning, when dawn was a whisper of pale gray on the horizon, he turned over in bed and discovered she wasn't beside him. He fought down a moment of panic before noticing that the pile of her discarded clothes on the floor was undisturbed. His shirt wasn't hanging from the back of the chair where he'd tossed it, though.

He got out of bed, pulled a pair of boxers from a drawer and put them on before walking out into the hallway. A light was on in the living room. He found her wearing his shirt and sitting on the old battered sofa holding a framed picture. He knew from the frame which picture it was, and his stomach clenched with anxiety.

"I missed you," he said, sitting beside her on the couch.

Still holding the picture in one hand, she put her other one on his thigh and snuggled closer. "Couldn't sleep."

He gazed at the artificially toned sepia photograph in its leather and wood frame. "That was a long time ago." He remembered the rollicking trip to Tombstone to watch the gunslingers in action on the streets during Helldorado Days. At the last minute Pete had decided to have an old-time picture taken of the five of them.

Ernie and Pete were posed stiffly in ladder-back chairs, dressed in a formal fashion so unlike their usual style, with elaborate coats, collars, cravats and stovepipe hats. The kids were more true to type. At eleven Mike had loved the role of gunslinger the photographer had given him. Alana had been cast as a Calamity Jane clone with six-shooters strapped to her hips. She'd insisted on standing next to Mike and had one arm possessively around his shoulders.

Beth, nine at the time, stood on the other side of the seated men. She wore a dress with a high collar and a bustle, and a feathered hat was perched on her head. She held an open parasol over one shoulder. In keeping with the photography style of that era, none of them were smiling. That in itself was unusual. Laughter had been a common sound when the five of them went adventuring together.

"She'll be here today," Beth said, staring at the picture.

"Probably."

"Mike, I don't want to tell her yet."

His hopes began to fade. "You'll only hurt her more if you don't tell her right away." His worst fear was that Beth would decide not to tell her at all, that she'd send him away and end their relationship.

"She has a lot to deal with, considering Ernie's blood clot and everything, and canceling her trip, and seeing you again after all these years. I just can't hit her with this first thing, Mike."

"And how long do you plan to wait?" he asked quietly.

She wouldn't look at him. "I don't know."

He took her chin between his fingers and turned her to face him. "We've had quite a time in the past few days," he said. "The pleasure has been incredible, but there's one thing that's been missing from all of it."

She looked uneasy, as if she knew good and well what was coming. "Mike, maybe it would be better if we postponed any discussions about us until after Alana gets home."

"I'm not interested in a discussion. But before this next day starts, before you leave this house, there is one thing you should know."

"No, Mike." She tried to twist away.

"Yes." He held her chin, forcing her to look at him. "I love you, Beth. Not as a brother, or as an old friend, but as a man, a man who feels complete every time he holds you, every time he pushes deep inside you."

Panic flooded her gaze. "You don't know what you're saying," she whispered. "Your father's condition has you all mixed up. You—"

"I know exactly what I'm saying. Does my father's condition have you all mixed up?"

"I—I have to wait until Alana gets here."

Sick disappointment assaulted him. "Alana has nothing to do with whether or not you love me."

"I know that, but somehow I have to see her before I...say anything to you."

"You mean you can make love to me all night, in every position imaginable, and that's okay, but you can't tell me you love me, because that's betraying your sister?"

"Mike, you don't understand."

He hurt, and he wanted her to hurt, too. "Oh, I understand all right. I understand that you haven't grown up, after all."

She twisted away from him and stood. "I'm getting dressed and going home."

He got to his feet. "I'll drive you."

"I'll walk."

"I'll *drive you*, dammit. Don't let stupid pride put you in the position of walking through the streets in last night's outfit. I know you, Beth. You'd regret it later."

"You're right. I accept the ride." She looked up at him,

tears in her eyes. "Please try to understand about Alana, Mike. She's all I've got!"

She couldn't have done more damage if she'd plunged a knife into him. He swallowed the lump of grief that rose to his throat. "The worst part is, I think you believe that."

12

THAT MORNING in the studio, Beth didn't even attempt to cut glass. The dentist's window would have to wait until she'd made it through this crisis. Instead she concentrated on the more mechanical work of applying copper foil to the edges of each section that had already been cut. Unfortunately the repetitive job left her mind free to replay the events of the night before.

Perhaps she'd lost Mike forever because she'd been unwilling to tell him what she'd known for years, that she loved him in a way that allowed no other man to claim her heart. The problem was, so did Alana. In Beth's mind, once she admitted her love to Mike, then she had chosen him over her sister. She wasn't ready to do that yet. She might never be ready to do that.

Mike could be right when he said she hadn't grown up. But he still had a father, while she had no one left in her family except Alana—the one who had taught her to tie her shoes and braid her hair, the one who had loaned her makeup before her father allowed her to have any, the one who had comforted her through her measles, strep throat and her first cramps. Mike was an only child who couldn't be expected to understand the bond between her and Alana, even though he'd said more than once that he did.

When the bell tinkled announcing someone coming into the gift shop, she put down the piece of glass she was foiling and went to investigate with some trepidation. It couldn't be Alana, who would have burst through the back door in a flurry of greetings. But it could be Mike. She didn't feel like having another discussion right now. Hoping to find a customer in the shop, she walked out of the workroom.

Colby Huxford stood next to the counter, a malevolent look in his eyes to match the jagged scab on his cheek. "Hello, Beth."

"Colby." She nodded but didn't offer her hand. "I hope your cheek hasn't caused you any problems." Belatedly she realized he might have been able to press charges, especially if the cut had required stitches.

"No, it hasn't been a problem." He set his briefcase on the counter and opened it. "But I do have something you might want to hear." He laid a small portable tape recorder on the counter and pushed the Play button.

Beth's first wild thought was that Colby had been sneaking around Mike's house recording them making love so that he could blackmail her. Yet he knew nothing about the problem with Alana, so that didn't make sense.

Colby's voice came on first. *"So you bought the Nightingale Glass Cutter for your son, Mrs. Eckstrom?"*

As Mrs. Eckstrom said that she had, Beth remembered giving Colby that reference to check because the Sierra Vista woman had been so excited about her teenager taking an interest in something artistic.

"Has he had any injuries as a result of using it?"

Beth's glance flicked up from the tape recorder to Colby's face as an alarm bell sounded in her head.

"Well, he sliced his finger the other day, if that's what you mean."

"With the cutter?" Colby asked.

"That's what he said."

"That's impossible!" Beth cried. "You can't cut yourself on that tool. On the glass, sure, but the tool? Never!"

"Did the injury cause any problems for your son?" Colby's questioning continued.

"Well, he couldn't pitch in the baseball tournament that day, and I heard there were scouts in the crowd, but they might not have been there. You never know."

"So your son might have missed out on a possible scholarship opportunity because of an injury caused by the Nightingale Cutter?"

"This is ridiculous!" Beth raged. "You're convincing her that she has a complaint. I'm sure he cut himself on a piece of glass and just didn't explain it right to his mother."

Colby pushed another button to rewind the tape. "I think you've heard enough. I did convince her, Beth. She's talking to a lawyer today and I'm sure he'll be contacting you. I had to call every single one of the customers you so kindly gave me the numbers for until I found someone with a problem, but I finally found one."

"You're wasting your time. I can demonstrate that the cutter wasn't responsible for his finger being cut. It scores glass. It doesn't slice it."

"Possibly. But you'll run up a fair amount of legal fees in the meantime, and Mrs. Eckstrom's lawyer may be able to get an injunction to prevent you from manufacturing any more until this is cleared up. Then there's the bad publicity that may get out. Most people don't know how a glass cutter works. They'll assume it could cause injury."

Beth glared at him as the implications of his behavior became obvious. Financially she and Ernie were stretched to the max. Even minor legal fees could run them into trouble, and an injunction plus bad publicity would be a disaster. "You lizard. You'd ruin me just for revenge."

"Heavens, no. I have a deal for you. If you'll sign over the rights to the patent under the terms I dictate, then Handmade will take care of this woman's claim. We have lawyers on retainer who are trained to deal with such things. We may have to pay her a little to keep her happy, but considering what we'll save on leasing the patent from you, it'll be a wash."

"I can prove that you provoked her into saying those things. It's right on that tape."

"I guess you didn't notice I pushed the Erase button a little while ago. That tape no longer exists."

"But Mrs. Eckstrom knows that you called her with leading questions! She—"

"She'd like some money to get her son started in college. And all I was doing was checking on the safety of the tool because my company is in the process of acquiring the patent. Nothing devious about that." He tossed the recorder back into his briefcase and shut it. "I'm at the White House Bed and Breakfast in Warren when you feel like talking about a deal. I wouldn't wait too long if I were you. When Mrs. Eckstrom's lawyer calls, you'll want to be able to refer the situation to Handmade's legal counsel, I imagine." He headed for the door.

"You know, I have an apology to make."

He turned, his gaze expectant. "That's more like it."

"A minute ago I called you a lizard."

He smirked at her. "And you'd like to apologize for that remark?"

"Yes. I'd like to apologize to every lizard in the world for the biggest insult I could have paid them! Now get out of my shop."

His face twisted in anger. "You'll regret your attitude, Beth, when it comes time to sign the contract. You'll get no quarter from me."

"I will *never* sign your blasted contract!" she called after him. But once he was gone, she wondered if she was just spitting in the wind. The scenario he'd outlined could mean the end of not only the cutter, but Nightingale-Tremayne, Inc. as well. She couldn't risk that.

The back door flew open with a bang. "Bethy, it's me!" shouted a familiar voice from the back hall. "Kill the fatted calf, or whatever the hell you're supposed to do at a time like this! Your big sister is in residence!"

MIKE FIGURED eventually he'd regret his outburst to Beth, and sure enough, by midmorning, as he was supervising the work of the two machinists from Sierra Vista, he began to feel like a jerk. He'd expected too much, too soon. Not so long ago he'd wondered if he'd even get a chance to make love to Beth at all, and within forty-eight hours he was demanding that she declare her feelings and broadcast their relationship to Alana.

His only excuse was his recent discovery that he was madly, passionately in love with Beth. That was a funny excuse for hurting the very person he claimed to love so much. Ernie had told him not to screw things up, but he was well on his way to doing just that with his impatience. He'd waited eight years to straighten out this mess. He could wait a little longer.

His instincts told him that it would be kinder to tell Alana immediately, but his instincts might be off. He'd rather get the bad news right away, but not everybody was the same. Beth knew Alana better than he did. Timing might be very important, and Beth wanted the freedom to choose the right time. Unless he wanted to alienate her completely, he'd better go along with that.

With two employees working with him on the cutters, he soon had a stack of boxes that gave him a reasonable excuse to drive over to Beth's studio. He thought of calling first, but decided he'd rather just appear and not give her time to think about things too much.

BETH WASN'T SURE it was a great idea to be drinking beer with Alana at eleven in the morning after getting practically no sleep the night before, but Alana was in a funky mood and had talked her into it. After hugs and hauling Alana's stuff upstairs, the two of them sat at the little table in the workroom while Beth filled Alana in on the Colby Huxford problem.

"What did you say the customer's name was, again?" Alana asked. She was dressed in typical Alana style—khaki shorts, a sleeveless, scoop-neck white T-shirt and hiking boots. Her sun-bleached blond hair was caught back with a leather barrette, and after a summer of outdoor activities, she was lean, tanned and glowing with the energy that always characterized her.

"Eckstrom," Beth said.

"From Sierra Vista, right?"

"Right."

Alana took a drink from her beer and then pointed the bottle at Beth. "It has to be the same family I took down to Havasu Falls last year. Remember how we decided to cross-pollinate our mailing lists for the two businesses?"

"Yeah, but so what if it is the same family? In fact, that might be bad, if they're connected to both of us. If they've become lawsuit-happy, they might decide you let them get sunburned on that trip and now they should be compensated for a greater risk of skin cancer."

"I don't think that'll happen, and I'll tell you why. That kid of theirs, the one they're now claiming missed his chance to try out for the big leagues, or however it's now being exaggerated, was into drugs last year."

"Seriously?"

"Seriously. Small stuff, like pot, but he was definitely hanging out with the wrong crowd and giving his parents fits. That hike into the canyon with his folks and his little brother turned him around." Alana drained her beer. "Not to be immodest, but *I* turned him around. I told him if he stayed clean I'd make room for him on my first expedition down the Amazon."

The Amazon. Beth felt queasy with guilt as thoughts of Mike and their secret washed over her.

"Hey, are you okay?" Alana leaned forward and put her hand on Beth's. "Maybe you shouldn't be drinking beer, after all."

Beth straightened in her chair and squeezed her sister's hand. "I'm fine. And congratulations for getting that kid on the right track. I had no idea that those trips could accomplish that kind of thing." The beer was definitely having an effect, Beth noticed. She remembered she hadn't eaten anything since dinner the night before, either, and she was becoming more light-headed by the minute.

"Get people outdoors, take away the normal distractions, force them to work together and all sorts of dynamics change. I could almost hire myself out as a family counselor. Anyway, I think we can use this kid's hopes for the Amazon to our advantage, don't you?"

Beth was having trouble following the discussion with the slight buzzing in her head. "I think we need a bag of chips." She stood up. Not a good move. But she needed food of some description, so she forced herself to start toward the hall and the stairs leading up to the apartment.

Alana leaped to her feet and put an arm around Beth's shoulders. "I'll get the chips," she said, guiding her back to her chair. "I'll bet you've been up all night cutting glass. You work too hard, Beth."

"Not really." Beth sank onto the chair with a little sigh of relief. She wondered how much more of this she could take. Every remark of Alana's stabbed her with guilt, yet she couldn't imagine how to broach the subject of Mike, especially while Alana was trying so hard to help her with Colby Huxford.

"Do you have any of that cheese dip, the kind with the picante sauce in it?" Alana called over her shoulder.

"I think there's some in the refrigerator."

"Great. This is fun, just like old times, the two of us brainstorming a problem and eating junk." She took the stairs at a rapid clip.

Beth rested her head in her hands and tried to think, but her brain wasn't working worth a darn. When the bell on the front door of the gift shop jangled, she considered hiding in the back and not acknowledging the summons. Whoever had come in would eventually leave. Of course they might leave with some of the merchandise, which she could ill afford if she was about to be sued.

With an effort she got up and walked out into the shop where Mike was just depositing a stack of boxed cutters on the counter. She'd forgotten he might show up. "Oh, Mike. I—"

"Don't say it." He crossed quickly to her and took her by the shoulders. "I was wrong. I shouldn't have pressured you. Can you forgive me for being a total idiot?"

She stepped away from him. "Listen—"

"Please don't push me away. I need you, Beth."

"Is that Mike Tremayne's voice I hear?" Alana skipped through the double doors of the workroom holding a bag of chips and a jar of cheese dip.

Mike spun away from Beth. "Well, hello there, Alana."

Alana plopped the chips and cheese dip on the counter next to the cutter boxes. "Hello there, Mike." She gave him a wide smile. "My goodness, you sure have turned into a gorgeous hunk of man."

"And you're even prettier than I remembered," Mike said, returning her smile.

"I like the way this conversation is starting out," Alana said. "Tell you what, I'm ready to forget the past if you are, and after all these years, I think I deserve at least a big hug." She came forward, arms outstretched.

Mike enfolded her in his arms. "You deserve a long overdue apology from me, for one thing. I was a rotten son of a bitch, Alana."

"I don't even want to discuss that business again. It's over and done. Welcome back, big guy."

Beth clenched her hands into fists and willed herself to stay calm when she wanted to forcibly pull her sister away from the man she loved. But of course Alana loved him, too. That much was obvious from the lingering way she hugged him. The trouble was, Mike didn't seem in a big hurry to let go of Alana, either.

At last Alana stepped back and turned to include Beth. "So. Here we all are again. Older, and let's hope, wiser. Come on back, Mike. We're having a beer and figuring out how to take care of this sleaze Huxford."

Mike glanced quickly at Beth. "What about Huxford?"

"Oh, he's talked one of Beth's cutter customers into

filing a lawsuit," Alana said without waiting for Beth to answer. "But I think we can outfox him. Come and have a beer with us, and we'll tell you all about it."

Mike sent another questioning look in Beth's direction.

She shrugged.

"Come on, Mikey. I have a cold one back here with your name on it." Alana linked her arm through his and started back toward the workroom. "You're looking so damned fit. I'll bet you drove those Brazilian girls crazy."

"The women of Brazil don't hold a candle to the women of Bisbee," Mike said.

Alana laughed. "That's my Mike."

Beth wanted to scream. She'd had no idea that Alana's behavior with Mike would rub her nerves raw, or that Mike would fall right back into the old pattern of flirting with Alana. She'd been so worried about Alana's reaction to her relationship with Mike that she'd ignored the price she'd pay for keeping silent. But if she was in pain, she had no one to blame but herself. She'd been the one who'd insisted that Alana shouldn't be told right away. Shy, careful Beth. She probably didn't deserve a guy like Mike.

Because there were only two chairs in the room, Mike leaned against Beth's workbench. He drank the beer that Alana opened for him while she told him the story of Colby's attempt to blackmail Beth into signing away the rights to the patent. Like the quiet, unobtrusive member of the trio she'd always been, Beth listened while Alana and Mike got into a spirited debate about how to handle the problem.

Then Mike broke the pattern by turning to Beth. "What do you want to do?" he asked.

Alana answered. "Of course she wants to—"

"I asked Beth," Mike interrupted. "This is her baby, after all."

Alana's glance flicked from Mike to Beth. "Well, *excuse* me."

"I'd rather scrap the whole damned project than turn it over to Colby Huxford," Beth said with a little more vehemence than she'd intended.

"Whoa, stand back!" Alana said. "I think little Bethy's mad!"

"Good for you," Mike said with an approving look.

"And if Alana's willing to use her influence with the Eckstroms, that's fine with me," Beth added.

"That's all I needed to hear." Alana popped up from her chair. "I'll just get in my little Jeep and take me a drive to Sierra Vista."

"I'll close the shop and come with you," Beth said.

"Then why don't we all go?" Alana asked, glancing at Mike. "We can leave from there and go on to Tucson to see Ernie."

"I think the two of you will do just fine without me along," Mike said. "Besides, I have a few loose ends to tie up here before I drive up to Tucson. I'll meet you at the hospital."

Alana shrugged. "Suit yourself. I can't imagine a man turning down a chance to take a drive with two such bodacious babes, but you do what you have to do, I guess."

Mike grinned. "Sacrifice builds character."

Beth glanced at him and at first saw only the bantering tease he'd always been when the three of them got together. But her senses were more finely tuned to his moods now, and a closer look revealed the faint line of tension between his eyebrows and the uncompromising set of his jaw. Something was on his mind, and it probably had to do with the "loose ends" he'd talked about taking care of. She would bet Colby was one of those ends.

"Don't do anything crazy," she said to him.

His grin flashed again. "I'm sitting with two women who started drinking beer at eleven in the morning, and one of them is warning *me* not to do anything crazy?"

"You know what I mean."

"I don't," Alana said, "and I hate it when I don't know what's going on."

Mike shot one look at Beth, but one look was more than enough. Alana had just said she hated not knowing what was going on. It was an opening anyone could drive a truck through—but Beth chose not to take it. When she told Alana about her involvement with Mike she wanted to be alone with her sister. Alana deserved at least that much consideration, that much respect for her pride.

"Okay, enough of the significant looks," Alana said to Beth, her tone impatient. "Tell me what you think Mike might do while we're in Sierra Vista."

"I think he might go beat the hell out of Colby Huxford," Beth said. "Then Colby will have him arrested for assault, and I...won't have anyone to run the machine shop and make the cutters," she concluded, putting everything on a business footing.

"I promise not to beat the hell out of Huxford," Mike said. "Although the idea is tempting."

"Will you promise to stay away from him?"

Mike gazed at her. "Nope."

"Mike, Alana's plan might very well work. Once we eliminate the blackmail element, Colby will just have to pack his bags and go home."

"I don't read him as the type to do that, unless he has some extra prodding."

"Like what? You promised not to lay a hand on him just now."

"And I'll keep that promise. We'll just talk."

"I don't like the sound of it."

"I do," Alana interjected. "Let Mike talk to him." She gazed up at him with an expression of frank admiration. "I'm sure he can be very convincing when he wants to be, right, Mike?"

Mike winked at her. "Absolutely. I'll see you two at the hospital around six-thirty."

ALANA ZIPPED UP her Jeep's windows and turned on the air-conditioning, although Beth suspected she'd have ridden to Sierra Vista with the Jeep open despite the summer heat if Beth weren't along.

"We'll stop before we go to the Eckstrom's, get a Big Mac or something and call to make sure somebody's there," Alana said, taking charge as she always had. "I think the mother, Sarah, will be around. She types medical transcripts at home to bring in extra money."

"I know she really wants her son to go to college, too," Beth said. "That's probably why she fell for this line of Colby's. You know, the idea that someone would hurt themselves on the glass and sue the manufacturer of the cutter never even occurred to me, Alana. I suppose it should have."

Alana reached over and patted her knee. "Not really. You just ran into a skunk. The cutter's perfectly safe, and you know it. In my case, I've been concerned about lawsuits ever since I started Vacation Adventures, Inc. You should see the premium on the insurance I have to pay to protect me in my business. Even so, I'm not sure I'd be covered if somebody died while I had them out on a trip."

"What a thought! Have you ever been afraid that might happen?"

"Oh, yeah! You can't predict exactly how things will go when you're hiking up and down mountains, or rafting down rapids. Accidents happen, although I try to take every precaution. And then there's the off chance that somebody will decide to have a heart attack out in the middle of nowhere."

"Ugh. It's bad enough when you can call the paramedics right away, like we did for Ernie."

"Is he really okay, Bethy? I know what the doctor said, but I never know if they're feeding me a line of bull or not. I've been so worried. I'm worried for Mike, too."

"Yeah, I know." Beth sighed. "It was pretty scary, but I think he's okay, now. We'll be sure in a couple more days."

"When did Mike show up?"

The question popped up as if it were a hand grenade in a bushel of apples. "A few days ago."

"Was he here when I called the other day?"

Beth refused to tell an outright lie. "Yeah. He'd just arrived."

"How come you didn't tell me about it?"

"I was afraid you'd come rushing back to see him. I thought your trip with the family was more important. But I realize now I should have told you and let you make that decision."

Alana glanced at her, but her eyes were hidden by the sunglasses she wore. "You're right. I probably would have come back. I'm tired of being alone, Beth. I'm thirty-two years old, and I'm ready to settle down with a guy. Not just any guy, either. I've been thinking about

Mike a lot, lately, and he's still the one for me. I've loved him ever since we were six, and I still do. The timing was off eight years ago, but did you see the way he looked at me? I think we can start over."

Pain surged through Beth. "Alana, I—"

"I know what you're going to say. He still wants to spend his time traveling, and he'll never want a house with a white picket fence around it. That's okay, because neither do I. That's why I'm going to make him a proposition. I want him to go into business with me. That way he can satisfy his wanderlust and be part of a growing enterprise at the same time. Think he'll consider it?"

"I guess you'll have to ask him." Truth be told, Beth was no longer positive that he'd reject the offer. It seemed tailor-made for him, as opposed to running a Brazilian glass studio. When she saw how easily he interacted with Alana, and she with him, they still seemed to be the perfect couple. Maybe they *were* the perfect couple, and Mike had clung to her because he was in the midst of an emotional time in his life. She pictured the humiliation of announcing to Alana that Mike was interested in her, now, and then discovering that he'd changed his mind.

She tried to tell herself such a thing would never happen. Mike loved her. He'd said so not very many hours ago. He'd made love to her all through the night. He wouldn't turn to Alana, now, would he?

Except that she hadn't returned his vows of love. She'd insisted on waiting, as if she were some little kid, until Alana came home. No wonder he'd accused her of not being grown up. And it would serve her right if he decided Alana was the woman she didn't have the guts to be. As Beth glanced at Alana driving the Jeep so confidently with one hand, her body lithe and fit in a way Beth had never aspired to, she wondered if the past few days had been a fantasy, after all.

13

AFTER TELLING his machinists to go grab some lunch, Mike made a quick trip home and then set out in search of Colby Huxford. He'd forgotten to ask Beth where the vermin was staying, but his first guess, the elegant White House Bed and Breakfast in Warren, turned out to be on target. Mike talked to the folks there and said he was interested in locating Huxford on some urgent business having to do with the glass cutter patent Huxford wanted to purchase from Beth Nightingale. With that kind of detailed lead-in, he easily got the information that Huxford was probably eating lunch at his favorite midday spot, a little Italian deli in the heart of Bisbee. Mike knew the place.

Before he walked in, he made sure Huxford was there by sauntering past the glass-fronted deli and glancing at the tables. Sure enough, the weasel sat chowing down on what looked like a salami sandwich. How Mike would have loved to go in and ram it down his throat. When he thought of Huxford threatening Beth this morning, he wanted to kill the son of a bitch. But he'd promised Beth he wouldn't be violent.

The minute he walked into the sandwich shop Huxford glanced up as if he were a wild animal scenting danger in the air. Mike walked over to Huxford's table, pulled out a chair and sat down.

"I'm afraid you're not invited to stay," Huxford said. His Adam's apple bobbed.

Mike took pleasure in his obvious fear. "I'm not staying. I'm here to deliver a message. By the way, that's an interesting scratch on your cheek there. Cut yourself shaving, did you?"

"Don't get cute with me, Tremayne. Did Beth send you?"

"No. In fact, Beth and her sister, Alana, are on their way to Sierra Vista to see the Eckstroms."

"I'd advise them to send a lawyer instead."

"I don't think they'll need one." Mike leaned his forearms on the marble-topped table and deliberately shoved himself into Huxford's personal space. "Alana took that family on an outdoor vacation last year and single-handedly turned the son from a potential drug addict into a high school sports star. The kid, and the parents, would do about anything for Alana. She's going to ask them to forget about this asinine suit you talked them into."

"We'll see." Huxford leaned back in his chair and flexed his shoulders in a comical show of bravado. "Mrs. Eckstrom seemed quite concerned about her son's future when I talked with her."

"Oh, I think this will work. Beth's going, too, and folks around Bisbee learned a long time ago that you don't mess with those Nightingale girls. The fact is they don't need me to drive the last nail in your coffin. They can take care of themselves. I'm here strictly for my own pleasure."

Huxford sneered. "I suppose you'll threaten to beat me up or something if I don't leave town by sundown."

"That would be fun, but I promised Beth I wouldn't

lay a hand on you. However, I do expect you to be gone by tonight."

"And if I'm not?"

Mike sat back in his chair and crossed his ankle over one knee. "Well, let me tell you a little about myself, Huxford."

"Not interested."

"You should be. Last year I got real chummy with a tribal shaman down in South America. The rain forest natives have herbal concoctions you've never heard of. Poisonous frogs are a big thing, too. The hunters tip their arrows with some stuff that's so lethal that one scratch will bring down a jaguar in seconds."

"So?" Huxford licked his lips in a nervous gesture.

Mike reached into his pocket and pulled out a small metal box. He opened the catch and put the open box on the table. "There wasn't a lot to do in the evenings in the rain forest. I got pretty good with a blow gun. I learned how to mount the arrows on the shaft, too. Attach them one way and they fly perpendicular to the ground, which is how they need to go if you want them to penetrate the ribs of an animal. Attach them so they fly horizontally, and they'll slide between the ribs of a man."

Huxford glanced around the shop. It was empty, and even the owners were busy back in the kitchen catching up on some delivery orders.

By the time he glanced back at the table, Mike had re-pocketed the box containing the arrowhead. "No witnesses, Huxford. There wouldn't be any when I hit you with the arrowhead, either."

"You're either bluffing or you're insane."

Mike smiled at him. "If I were you, I wouldn't hang around a town with a potential madman in it. Could be dangerous to your health."

Huxford pushed out of his chair, leaving most of his sandwich on the plate in front of him. "I've heard enough of your crap." He threw some money on the table. "I begged the company not to send me out to this godforsaken place. You can have it." With that he stomped out of the deli.

"Thanks. Believe I will," Mike said to the empty room. He picked up the untouched half of Huxford's sandwich and began to eat.

BECAUSE HE WASN'T squiring Beth and Alana around, Mike decided to take his dad's old truck to Tucson. Storm clouds had been threatening for the last couple of days, but tonight they looked really serious. He wondered if Alana's Jeep leaked during a downpour. If it did, the two women would probably get wet on the return drive to Bisbee.

Then again, maybe he'd be taking Beth home in the truck and Alana would be driving back to Phoenix. He couldn't believe she'd want to hang around once Beth broke the news. He hoped to hell she'd done it by now, even if that meant the visit to Ernie's room wouldn't be all sweetness and light. It was time to get things out in the open.

He couldn't exceed the speed limit in the aging truck as he had in the rental car, and he was running late. By the time he arrived at the hospital, big drops of rain pelted the asphalt parking lot. The air smelled of damp creosote bushes, a tangy fragrance peculiar to the desert that Mike happened to love. Thunder growled over the mountains. It would be a wet night.

When he started down the hall toward Ernie's room, he found Alana and Beth waiting together in the hall. One look at their untroubled expressions told him that

Alana still knew nothing. Disappointment ate away at the glow of triumph he felt from his encounter with Huxford.

Nevertheless he approached the two women and put a smile on his face. He'd have to continue to play this Beth's way. "What's up?"

"The doctor's with him and asked us to step outside for a minute," Alana said. "Your shirt's damp. Must be raining out there."

"Yep. How'd the discussion go with Mrs. Eckstrom?"

Alana grinned. "She doesn't think she wants to pursue that lawsuit, after all. Turns out her son did cut himself on the glass, not on the tool, but he wanted to blame something besides his own carelessness, so he said the cutter did it."

"We even got the cutter out and ran it back and forth across everybody's hand to prove the point," Beth added. "Mrs. Eckstrom apologized for putting us through all the trouble."

"That's terrific." Mike looked into Beth's eyes and wasn't encouraged. The strong glow of love and passion that had been there the night before had dimmed considerably. He could see the whole thing pretty clearly— Alana had charged in to save the day and Beth couldn't bring herself to lower the boom on Alana's fantasies. But where that left him wasn't at all clear.

"Okay, your turn," Alana said. "What happened when you saw Huxford?"

"Well, I told him you two were punching a large hole in his lawsuit scheme."

"Our counterattack might not have worked, you know," Beth reminded him.

"I knew it would work. As I told Huxford, anybody

who's lived around Bisbee very long knows that when the Nightingale girls join forces, watch out."

Alana laughed. "So once you told him we were on the case, he turned tail and ran back to Chicago?"

"Not quite. But he is gone."

Beth looked worried. "Mike, you promised not to get physical."

Mike put up both hands. "I didn't hit him. Not even once. It took a lot of restraint, but the only mark on that slimeball is the one you put there."

Alana stared at her sister. "*Beth* hit this guy? This I have to hear."

Mike listened to Beth's abbreviated version of why she slapped Huxford. As he expected, she left out Huxford's remark that Mike had gotten there ahead of him sexually. She left out the fact that she'd met Huxford as she returned home after spending several hours in a hotel bed with Mike.

"Awesome, sis," Alana said. "I can't believe you got violent so quickly, just because he tried to make a move on you. You must be getting feistier in your old age. It's too bad, in a way, that he wasn't a nice guy." She turned to Mike. "Which reminds me. We need to have a talk with this girl, Mike. She's tucked herself away in her studio down in Bisbee, where she hardly ever meets single guys. I've tried to get her to spend time with me in Phoenix so I could introduce her around, but she won't come. I worry that she's going to become a shriveled-up old maid type who putters in her glass studio and has no life."

Mike fixed Beth with a relentless gaze, taking no pity on her just because her cheeks were growing pink. "Is that what's going to happen to you, Beth?" he asked softly.

She sent him a challenging glance. "I think we're getting off the subject of what you said to Colby."

"Yeah, I'm curious about that, too," Alana said.

So Mike filled them in on the conversation at the deli and watched Beth's eyes grow wide with disbelief.

Finally the tension must have overwhelmed her, because she grabbed his arm. "I hope to God you don't really carry around a poison-tipped arrowhead that would kill somebody!" Then she withdrew her hand quickly, as if she'd touched a hot stove.

The brief grip of her fingers was enough to make him long to pull her into his arms. One kiss in front of Alana would be worth a thousand words. But he didn't dare give in to that impulse and risk losing everything. "No, I don't have a poison-tipped arrowhead," he said. "I have no interest in carrying around something like that." He winked at her. "Especially with my reputation for being a little clumsy sometimes."

"So what was it you showed Huxford?" Alana asked.

"Just an arrowhead I brought home from Brazil. It *could* be tipped with poison, but it isn't. And I never told him it was. I just showed it to him after describing my expertise with a blow gun. He checked out of the White House B and B pretty quick after that, according to the person I talked to."

Alana chuckled. "That's great, Mike."

"Can you really use a blow gun?" Beth asked, still visibly shaken from the story.

"Yeah, I can. It didn't take much practice, considering all the years I shot spit wads in school. It's the same principle." He gazed deliberately at Beth. "The secret's in how you use your tongue."

Beth's color heightened and she looked away, but Alana didn't seem to notice a thing. "I remember the time you shot a spit wad at me when we were taking the English final from old man Geddes," she said. "He almost flunked you."

"And you talked him out of it," Mike added, returning his attention to Alana.

"I should have let you hang," Alana said with a grin, "considering that was the same day you—"

"You can go in, now," the nurse said from the doorway of Ernie's room.

"Oh. Thanks, we will," Alana said, starting immediately for the room.

Mike took the opportunity to grab Beth by the shoulders. He held onto her until Alana was inside the door of Ernie's room. Then he leaned down and put his lips close to the side of her neck. "I love you, even if you are a coward," he murmured before biting her ever so gently.

She drew in a sharp breath but didn't turn in his direction. After he released her, she straightened as if she were a well-trained soldier and walked into the room. Feeling more discouraged than ever, Mike followed.

BETH REMEMBERED hating seesaws when she was a kid because the bouncing up and down made her stomach hurt. That's how she felt now. One minute she couldn't imagine devastating Alana by telling her about Mike, and the next she was dying of frustration and ready to shout out the news. In between these bouts she watched Mike and Alana interact and couldn't help noticing how alike in temperament they were. For most of her life she'd believed they should be together. They were the strong ones, the brave ones. She was the little mouse who yearned for excitement but didn't have the nerve to claim the life she wanted.

With the imprint of Mike's gentle nip burning as if it were a brand on her skin she walked into Ernie's room. Alana had already claimed the chair by his bed and was talking animatedly to him.

Ernie glanced up as Beth came in followed by Mike. There was an unmistakable question in his eyes. "So you're all in the same room together again," he said. "About time."

"Life's too short to hold grudges," Alana said, turning toward Mike. "Right?"

"Right," Mike responded.

"How are you feeling?" Beth asked, coming to the foot of the bed.

"Tip top, now that you three are all here."

"Nifty jaguar tooth you're wearing," Beth said, as she tried to tell herself Ernie was looking better, even though in her heart she knew he looked more tired than ever.

"Yeah, the nurses are callin' me Crocodile Dundee," Ernie said with a smile.

"Wait'll you see a jaguar in the wild, Dad," Mike said, moving up beside Beth, his body just barely touching hers. "It's an awesome sight."

Beth knew she should move away, but the underlying note of anxiety in Mike's voice made her stay near him. She could tell he was worried, too.

"I'll just bet it is," Alana said, turning toward Mike. "By the way, I was just telling your dad about my new brainstorm. I told Beth about it earlier, but the funny thing is that I haven't told you, and you're the key party in this."

"In what?"

Standing so close beside him, Beth felt Mike tense. She gripped the end rail of the hospital bed as a premonition of disaster swept over her.

"I think you should come into business with me," Alana said. "I've tapped into a lucrative market, and I need a good sidekick who's up for adventure and travel. I've been wanting to expand into rain forest treks for families. Your life-style would be about the same as it is now, but you'd be building something for yourself, financially. What do you think?"

In the agonized few seconds of silence that followed, Beth wished a tornado would come through and suck her right out of the room. That almost seemed like a possibility with the way the rain pounded against the window and lightning crackled outside.

"It's a gully-washer," Ernie remarked.

"Looks like it," Beth agreed.

"Well, Mike?" Alana prompted. "This business is really going places. I'd like you to be part of it."

"It's an interesting idea," Mike said at last. "I'll give it some thought."

"She might make you live in Phoenix," Ernie said.

"Oh, I know Mike wouldn't want to live in a big city," Alana said quickly. "That wouldn't be a requirement." She gazed at Mike. "Just promise me you'll think about it, okay?"

"Okay," he agreed, his tone neutral. "And I appreciate the offer."

"We'll consider it a standing one," Alana said. "You'd be good at this, Mike."

"Maybe so." He cleared his throat. "Listen, you haven't had as much time with Ernie as Beth and I have recently. Why don't you stay here and tell him about your canoe trip while Beth and I go out in the hall and talk? Something came up today at the shop about the cutter design, and I want to ask her a few things so I'm clear about the process for tomorrow."

"Sure," Alana said. "It's hard for me to picture you laboring away in that machine shop, though."

"I've sort of enjoyed it, to tell you the truth."

"Then you've changed a lot, Mike."

"I probably have, at that. Come on, Beth. Let's let them swap tall stories while you and I get some business accomplished." He took her arm and led her out of the room and several feet down the hall.

"How long have you known about this idea of Alana's?" he asked her once they were out of hearing range.

"She just mentioned it this afternoon." Beth gazed up at him, her stomach a nervous twist. "To be honest, it sounds perfect for you."

"There you go again, assuming you know what will make me happy. But I can tell you that this isn't it."

"Why not?"

He took her by both elbows. "Because I'd be dealing with the wrong sister, that's why not. Because I've always loved you, and you've always loved me, and it's finally dawned on me that I can have you and my adventures in the rain forest. You can have me and your stained-glass studio. We can make it all work—marriage, travel, children, happily ever after. That doesn't fit too well with being a partner in Alana's business."

Her chest felt tight. "You want to m-marry me?"

"Somebody should." He smiled down at her. "Or you're liable to turn into a shriveled-up old maid type who putters in her glass studio and has no life."

"But I'm too quiet, and I think too much about everything! Alana's like you, decisive and ready for action."

"Maybe that's why she's never excited me very much. I love those differences of yours. Alana's passion is all on the outside, for everybody to see. Yours is hidden away, and I'm the only man who knows just how deep it runs.

I've been fascinated by the rain forest because it's secluded and mysterious. I'm even more fascinated by the mysteries of Beth."

She began to tremble, and her heartbeat sounded loud in her ears.

"I can read your answer in your eyes," he murmured. "All you have to do is say it."

"Oh, Mike. It sounds so wonderful, but—"

"Of course, sometimes you do think too damn much," he muttered. He pulled her to her tiptoes and settled his mouth over hers.

"Beth," Alana called.

Beth quickly whirled away from Mike, but the minute she saw Alana's face, she knew it hadn't been quickly enough.

14

BETH REMEMBERED how Alana had looked when their father died, as if she'd imploded and all her energy had been sucked out, leaving a lifeless shell. She looked the same way now. Beth ran toward her, but Alana backed up, her expression bleak.

"Stay away!" Alana took another step backward. "Don't come near me! Neither of you!"

"I tried to think of how to tell you!" Beth cried out. "I didn't know how!"

Alana shook her head, as if to deny what she'd seen. She continued backing down the hall, and a nurse had to sidestep her in order to avoid a collision.

"We have to talk!" Beth pleaded, edging forward.

"No." The sound was a hoarse croak, barely audible. Then Alana turned and bolted down the hall.

Numbed by Alana's rejection, Beth could only stare helplessly after her.

Mike grabbed Beth's arm. "Come on. We have to go after her."

Beth hung back. "But she doesn't want us."

"That doesn't matter. It's pouring outside. If she decides to drive—"

"You're right." Fear chilled her blood. "You're faster. Go catch up to her. I'll tell Ernie we'll be back in a minute."

As Mike sprinted down the hall, Beth leaned in

through the doorway of Ernie's room. He was staring out into the hall, his expression worried, and she wondered how much he'd heard of what had taken place. "Something's come up," she said. "We'll be right back."

"Don't let anybody get hurt," Ernie said.

Too late, Beth thought, but she reassured Ernie anyway. "We won't." Then she ran down the hall after Mike.

ERNIE LISTENED to her run down the hall and closed his eyes in weary frustration. "The kids need help, Pete. Whatcha got for me?"

I'll keep an eye on them. Still don't know if I'll be able to do a darned thing except watch. I filled out all the applications, but nobody's approved anything.

"Danged red tape. I feel like just getting up out of this bed. But I think they took my clothes."

There's only one way you can leave that hospital tonight and do them any good. And nobody'll let me see the schedule, so I don't have the foggiest idea what's happening.

"Don't anybody up there understand we got us a crisis?"

I don't know, buddy. I'll keep trying.

BETH DIDN'T SEE Mike in the lobby but finally she spotted him standing beneath the overhang outside the main entrance. The heavy rain had created a waterfall in front of him.

She hurried out to join him. "Where is she?"

"I lost her. I got caught behind three people in wheelchairs and by the time I got out here she'd disappeared. I didn't know which way to go because I didn't know where you'd parked."

"Over there." Beth pointed in the direction of where

she remembered leaving the Jeep. "Mike, I see her! She's pulling out, right there!"

"You're right." He grabbed her hand. "The truck's not too far from there. Come on."

They ran through a downpour that soaked them to the skin in seconds. Beth splashed through puddles, sending sprays of water up her bare legs. And all the while she kept glancing at the Jeep headed for the parking lot exit. Fortunately a car had pulled out in front of Alana, which slowed her down.

"Keep an eye on her," Mike said. "See which way she turns while I get the truck started."

Beth's hopes faded. "You brought that old clunker? We'll never catch her in that!"

He unlocked the door and flung it open. "It's all we've got."

As he tried to coax the sputtering engine to life, Beth eased around to the passenger side while still watching Alana, who'd made it to the exit. When Beth heard the engine catch and the lock click open on the passenger door, she leaped inside. "East on Grant," she said.

Mike headed for the exit. "See if you can tell whether she turns right on Craycroft."

As Mike pulled out onto Grant, Beth could see the Jeep go straight through the intersection at Craycroft. "She's still driving east."

"Then she's not heading for the freeway. Which means she's not bound for either Phoenix or Bisbee. I wonder where the hell she's going?"

"She may not even know herself," Beth said quietly. "After Dad died, she drove out into the desert. I tried to follow her, but I didn't have four-wheel-drive, so she lost me. Finally she came back hours later and wouldn't talk to me about it. The next day she admitted not even remembering where she went. She just spaced the whole drive."

"Great." Mike barreled east on Grant toward the Rincon Mountains as lightning slashed through the clouds and thunder rolled overhead. "Let's hope traffic's held her up."

Beth peered through the heavy rain. The advancing darkness wasn't helping, either, but at least the Jeep was distinctive. At last she spotted it. "There!" She pointed out the Jeep. "Get in the left lane. She's turning on Tanque Verde."

"Okay." Mike glanced in his rearview mirror. "Damn, but I can't tell who's behind me in this glop." He rolled down his window and stuck his head out to check when it was safe to change lanes. By the time they made the turn they were two cars behind Alana.

"Assuming we can get behind her, how will we get her to pull over?" Beth asked. "She won't want to."

"I'm working on that." Thunder rumbled over the mountains ahead of them. "If the shoulder looks decent, I may try to force her off the road."

"Oh, Mike. That sounds too dangerous."

"So is driving spaced out through a rainstorm. We need to get her out of that Jeep."

"You shouldn't have kissed me!"

"You should have told her right away!"

She shouted to be heard over another peal of thunder. "I couldn't! You saw the way she leaped in to save me on the lawsuit thing! How could I tell her we were involved, after that?"

His voice rose a notch. "How could you let her think I would want to work for her?"

"How did I know you didn't?"

"Because I love *you*, dammit! And I wish you'd get it through your thick skull!"

"*I* have a thick skull? How about—Mike! She's going around that delivery truck."

"I see her. Hang on." Mike whipped the wheel to the right, and the truck fishtailed as he worked to keep the Jeep in sight.

"Can you catch up to her?"

"I've got it floored."

Beth groaned as another bolt of lightning lit up the sky. "If only you'd brought the rental car."

"How did I know I'd be involved in a high-speed chase?" He swore under his breath.

"Just swear out loud, Mike. I've heard all those words. From you, as a matter of fact. You taught them to me when we were kids, remember?"

"And that's about how we sound, arguing like this."

The temperature had plummeted with the coming of the rain, and Beth began to shiver in her wet clothes. "I wish we were still kids, and we were chasing Alana on our bikes, instead."

Mike flicked on the truck's heater. "We might as well be, as fast as this truck is. Thank God. She just got a red light. That'll help."

"I don't know how many more lights there are on this road. It's starting to get pretty desolate out here." Beth rubbed her arms to work away the goose bumps. "What if she takes off cross-country?"

The set of Mike's jaw became more determined. "We'll follow as long as we can, until we get stuck in mud or break an axle or blow a tire." He braked the truck as it came up behind Alana's Jeep at the light. "I'm going to honk the horn and let her know we're back here. Maybe she'll realize this is ridiculous and pull over."

"I doubt it, but go ahead and try."

Mike tapped the horn twice.

"I can't see her very well through that plastic window," Beth said. "Especially with the rain all over it."

"But she sees us, I'll bet."

Like a shot the Jeep spun away from the intersection.

"Damn! She ran the light!" Mike looked quickly both ways and stepped on the gas. "Too bad we weren't lucky enough to have a cop catch her doing that."

"I guess you have your answer as to whether she'll just pull over once she knows we're here."

"Crazy woman," he muttered, shifting quickly through the truck's gears.

"I *knew* she was going to react like this. I just knew it."

"Yeah, and I kept hoping you were exaggerating."

"Think about it from her standpoint, Mike. She's had her heart set on you since she was six years old. She said that today, in fact. You didn't tell her you weren't in love with her. You just left. That meant she was free to imagine anything, like, for example, that you'd get over your wanderlust and come home to her."

"That's true, but we could have cleared up that misconception as soon as she came home this time."

"We should have. I see that now, and it's my fault."

He reached over and gave her knee a quick squeeze. "It's been tough for you."

"I should have been braver about this."

"You might have been, if you'd really believed how much I love you."

She remained silent as she watched the taillights of the Jeep disappear into a dip in the road. The truck and the

Jeep were the only two vehicles on this lonely stretch, and Alana seemed to be gaining ground.

Mike glanced at her. "You're still having trouble with that concept, aren't you?"

"I saw you break Alana's heart," Beth said carefully. "I don't want you to do the same thing to mine." She noticed that way out here on the desert the thunder seemed louder, the lightning more savage. She shivered.

"I broke her heart because I've always been in love with you. Nothing about you and me is the same as it was with Alana and me. Nothing."

"Except that we've both been in love with you for years."

Mike gave her a sharp glance. "So you have been in love with me for years? You never admitted that before."

"I never wanted you to know. It made me too vulnerable."

His voice grew husky. "Be vulnerable for me, Beth. I swear I won't hurt you. You said you've loved me for years. For God's sake tell me you love me now."

"I— " She stopped speaking as the Jeep's taillights glowed brighter in the distance. "Mike! I think she's putting on her brakes."

"Looks like it. Hot dog. Maybe she's sick of this roller-coaster ride."

"No, I think it's the wash up ahead that made her stop. Look at the current of that water going across the road. Nobody's been out here yet to put up barricades, but that doesn't look passable to me. I'll bet she's deciding whether or not to drive through."

"She sure as hell better not. That's a bad crossing if I ever saw one. Listen, when we get closer to her, I'm going to swing the truck sideways across the road, to block her in case she tries to double back."

"I can't believe she'd drive through that wash," Beth said, trying to convince herself.

As they drew closer Beth estimated that the Jeep sat about ten feet from the edge of the stream that churned over the road. The Jeep's headlights illuminated the gray water, swift and filled with debris, but gauging its depth was impossible. A pack rat clung to a paloverde branch that swirled past.

"She's always talking about the fools who underestimate a desert wash when it's running," Beth said. "She knows it would be dumb to try. Even four-wheel-drive wouldn't guarantee anything."

"I hope she's remembering all that. Well, here goes." He slowed the truck and swung it in a wide arc to the left so it blocked both lanes.

Even before the truck stopped completely Beth opened her door and jumped out into the rain. She ran toward the Jeep, but before she could get there, it lurched forward, headed for the stream.

"No!" Beth screamed, running faster. "Alana, don't!"

The Jeep plowed into the water, sending geysers up past the tires. Beth didn't stop running or shouting until she was ankle-deep in water and almost lost her footing.

Mike grabbed her and yanked her back. "What're you going to do, hold onto the bumper?" he yelled into her ear.

Beth opened her mouth, but all that came out were ragged sobs. She swiped at the rain and tears in her eyes so she could watch the progress of the Jeep. *Please let her make it*, she prayed.

The Jeep moved steadily forward as the water lapped at the hubcaps. So far, so good. Then, abruptly, the right front tire plopped into a hole. The Jeep rocked and began to tilt.

"Oh, God," Mike said.

"Hang on!" Beth shouted, her throat raw.

The water shoved at the precariously balanced Jeep with increasing force. It tilted farther to the right.

"Maybe there's a rope in the truck bed." Mike released his grip on her arm and ran back to the truck.

Beth stood with her hands pressed to her mouth. Tears and rain coursed down her cheeks as the Jeep gave way to the rushing water and with a sickening splash went over on its side.

Mike's voice was frantic. "Can't find the damned rope!" he called. "I'll keep looking!"

The window unzipped, and Alana peered out. A sudden flash of lightning made her eyes glitter in her white face.

"Don't worry, we'll get you!" Beth screamed.

"Have you got a rope?" Alana yelled back.

"Mike's looking!"

The tow rope's under the danged seat, said a voice right beside her that sounded exactly like Ernie's.

Beth spun in the direction of the voice.

Ernie stood about six feet away from her, his cigar jammed in the corner of his mouth, his Western shirt and scruffy jeans remarkably dry. The jaguar tooth was no longer around his neck. *Tell him where the rope is,* Ernie said. *He ain't gonna find it on his own. He's too rattled.*

Beth kept her attention on Ernie. "The...the rope's under the seat!" she managed to call out as she stared at Ernie. The rain was still coming down in torrents, but he wasn't getting wet. An icy finger of premonition slid up Beth's spine. "How did you get here?" she whispered.

Never mind that. Just marry that boy of mine.

"I—"

Promise me, now, Beth. I ain't got all day to hang around.

"I promise, but—"

"I found the rope!" Breathing hard, Mike loped up beside her.

"Mike..."

"Okay, here's what we'll do." He handed her the end of the heavy nylon rope. "Tie this end to the truck. Get underneath and tie it to the axle. While you're doing that I'll get as far out as I can and throw it to Alana. She can tie it to the roll bar."

"Okay." Swallowing the lump in her throat, she hurried over to the truck, but once there she had to check the place where Ernie had been standing. Mike moved quickly past the spot without stopping. Her heart twisted in agony. As she'd expected, Ernie was gone.

She squirmed under the truck, grit from the road biting into her bare arms and legs, and tied the rope firmly to the front axle. By the time she wriggled out again, Alana was tying the other end to the roll bar as she balanced on the side of the Jeep. Mike stood knee deep in the water, and he staggered once as a piece of driftwood hit him in the back of the knees.

"Mike, come back a little!" she called as she started toward him.

"I'm okay! Once Alana's got the rope tied, I'll hang on to it."

The rope grew taut.

"It's tied!" Alana called.

"I'm coming out to get you!" Mike yelled back.

That was the moment Beth heard the soft but unmistakable sound of the truck moving slightly.

Set the emergency, Ernie said.

She looked around, but this time there was nobody

standing there. She ran toward the truck, leaped in and put on the emergency brake.

Now get some big rocks and put 'em beside the front and back tires.

She hurried to do it, barely having time to notice that Mike was up to his chest in swirling water as he worked his way down the rope toward Alana. She heaved up rocks she'd never dream of trying to lift otherwise. For some reason, they weren't as hard to carry as she'd thought, almost as if somebody was helping her with them.

That should do 'er, at least for the time bein'.

She ran to the water's edge and stood there panting as Alana climbed out of the Jeep onto Mike's back. Carrying Alana piggyback, Mike started working himself back along the rope. Once he stumbled, and Beth cried out.

Don't worry. He's gonna make it.

Beth swallowed. "He has to. I love him so much." She stood rigidly waiting as Mike reached the point where the water was at his waist, then his hips. Finally, when it was at his knees, Alana took hold of the rope and climbed down in front of him. When she reached ankle depth, Beth waded in and took her into her arms.

"I'm sorry," Alana sobbed. "I always knew he loved you. I thought I could beat you out. I almost d-did, too. But then you bought that d-damned red dress."

Beth held tight to her sister and cried with her for all the years of deceit and competition that had raged unacknowledged alongside their incredible love for each other. At last she heaved a ragged sigh. "It's over now. We're going to be okay."

"Yep," Alana said with a watery laugh. "Nobody messes with the Nightingale sisters."

"Nope," Beth said, giving her a big hug. "Not even us."

15

A RANCHER WITH A WINCH on the front of his dual-wheeled truck arrived soon after Mike rescued Alana. Mike and the rancher managed to get the Jeep upright and started hauling it back onto firm ground.

"Too bad that guy didn't show up sooner," Alana said. She and Beth sat in the cab of Ernie's old truck while they waited for the men to finish pulling the Jeep out. The rancher had given them a blanket and they'd wrapped it around themselves as they huddled together in the darkness.

"I think it's better he didn't show up until now," Beth said.

"I guess you're right." Alana tucked the blanket more firmly around them. "When Mike risked his life to save me and you were ready to leap into the water to swim out to get me, I was able to see what a jerk I was for putting us all in danger."

"You were furious with us and couldn't think straight."

"I know, but I didn't show much maturity in the way I reacted. While Mike was looking for the rope and my chances were getting slim, I realized how much the three of us mean to each other. I saw how dumb I was to give up the two people who loved me most in this world just because of wounded pride."

"Only pride?"

Alana sighed. "I hate to admit that. But the truth is, I've always loved Mike like a brother. I wanted him mostly because he was the best catch around, and it fed my ego to be able to say he was my boyfriend, my fiancé. Especially when I knew you wanted him, too."

"You *knew* that?"

Alana reached up and punched her gently on the shoulder. "What do you take me for? Stupid?"

"I thought I was keeping it a big secret."

"Oh, sure. Like the way you'd challenge him to wrestling matches all the time, and always be around when he came to pick me up, and then that red dress, my God. You might as well have taken out a billboard advertisement. No wonder he finally kissed you that night."

Beth's cheeks warmed. "You knew about *that*, too?"

"I saw you. That was one hot kiss. Mike and I never had that kind of chemistry, which is why it was no big deal for us to do the celibacy-before-marriage thing. I was ready to kill you that night, but bringing everything out in the open seemed like it would make the link between you two real, and I didn't want it to be. I figured I'd fight fire with fire and tried to seduce him later that night. As you know, it didn't work."

Beth had accepted Mike's version of that story, but it still didn't hurt his credibility to have Alana confirm the truth. "You wanted me to hate him."

"Sure I did. If you knew the truth, you might end up with him. Since you were already Dad's favorite, I didn't think that was fair."

"Dad's favorite?" Beth stared at her sister. "What makes you think a crazy thing like that?"

"Why wouldn't you be? You worked with him every day in the glass studio, and I wasn't any good at that. He was always bragging about your creativity. I always felt like...an outsider."

"Oh, Alana." Beth hugged her tight. "You know what Dad talked about when we worked together? He talked about you! How smart you were, and brave. *That girl's going to see every corner of the world someday,* he'd say, and his eyes would be shining with pride."

"You're making this up to make me feel better."

"I'm not. Cross my heart and hope to die, stick a needle in my eye. I used to be so jealous of *you* when he said that."

Alana chuckled. "God, Bethy, were we a pair or what? Hating each other and loving each other desperately at the same time. Each of us trying to be number one with Dad. I figured I'd lost that contest, so I made sure I had Mike, even though he really belongs with you."

Beth leaned her head against Alana's. "You're sure you're okay with that?"

"It's a relief, in a way. I've struggled so long to deny the attraction between you two. It was exhausting. I'm glad to finally give it up."

"So you've always known what the stained-glass piece in my studio was all about."

Alana nodded. "Many times I was tempted to have some *accident* happen to that piece, but it's so beautiful that even in my most jealous moments I couldn't destroy it. I didn't think either of us would get another shot at Mike, anyway, but when I heard he was back, and knew you'd spent time with him, I was like a fire horse hearing the bell. I had to get back here and try to get him, or at the very least keep you from getting him."

"That's amazing."

"It's stupid, is what it is. And he doesn't even turn me

on, at least not the way a guy should if you plan to spend your life with him."

"Then why haven't you fallen for somebody else?"

"More stupidity." She laid her head back against the worn upholstery. "I really need a shrink. I thought if I let myself become seriously involved, maybe even get married, then I wouldn't be available if Mike did come back. And you might be. You married to Mike would be such a blow to my ego that I had to guard against that horrible possibility at all times."

"And now your worst nightmare will come true."

"Now that it's here, it feels just right. Everything's the way it should be, with two people I love getting together at last. After all, you're the only family I've got—you, Mike and Ernie."

Ernie. Beth thought of what she'd seen and heard tonight. She wondered if she should tell Alana about it. If she did, she'd also have to tell Alana what she thought it meant. She could be wrong. The strain of the moment might have caused her to imagine something, to hallucinate. She'd read about such things, and maybe she'd just experienced the kind of tricks the mind could play when under tremendous stress.

Maybe she'd known herself where the rope was, and she'd only thought Ernie had been standing there telling her about it. The emergency brake was a logical thing to think of, and so were the rocks. If they'd seemed lighter than they should have been when she carried them, that was probably due to the sort of adrenaline rush that allowed mothers to lift cars away from their trapped children and not to some ghostly presence lightening the load.

She'd be foolish to describe what she'd seen and get Mike and Alana all excited and worried for nothing.

"You know, when I was in the Jeep, I thought I heard Dad's voice," Alana said.

Beth's head snapped around toward her sister. "What?"

"I couldn't be sure, and the water and thunder were making a lot of noise, but I thought I heard him say *You're all going to be okay.*" Alana's voice became choked with emotion. "I...um...probably imagined it."

Beth felt her own throat constrict with impending tears. "Maybe not."

"I want to believe he talked to me, Bethy," Alana whispered.

"Then believe it," she murmured, and swiped the tears from her cheeks. If their father really had talked to Alana, then maybe Ernie had really talked to her. "We...we need to go back to the hospital after the guys finish with the Jeep."

"Yeah, we sure do. Poor Ernie must wonder what all the fuss was about. Here he finally gets us together again after eight long years, and then all hell breaks loose. But I don't think we should tell him how dangerous it was."

"Probably not." Beth swallowed. "But he might know."

"Yeah, not much gets past Ernie. I love that old guy. When he gets better I'm taking him on a canoe trip with me. The Ozarks were beautiful. Maybe he'd like to go there."

Beth let the tears slide silently down her cheeks and prayed that Ernie would indeed see the Ozarks with Alana and the rain forest with his son.

Mike opened the driver's door. "I think that's about it," he said. "We're going to leave the Jeep here if it's okay with you, Alana. Jonas offered to pull it into town, but I think he's done plenty for us already, so I said we'd arrange for a tow in the morning, after the rain stops."

"Sounds fine to me," Alana said. "Considering we're all alive, I don't care what happens to the Jeep."

"It'll need some major time in the shop. There's sand in the engine."

"Who cares?" Alana said.

"I agree," Mike said. "I'll get Jonas's address and phone number so we can find him when we think up some way to say thank-you."

"Maybe he needs a stained-glass window in his ranch house," Beth suggested.

Mike smiled at her. "He just might. Well, I'll tell him goodbye and we'll be on our way."

"Beth and I want to go back to the hospital and let Ernie know we're okay," Alana said.

"Yeah, I thought we'd do that." Mike glanced at the two of them. "Although when he gets a look at us, he may not believe a word we say. You look like a couple of drowned rats, and I'm probably not much more attractive."

"Not much more attractive?" Alana glanced at Beth. "Did you hear what this egomaniac just said?"

"Yep." Beth laughed through her tears.

"Listen, Tremayne," Alana said, shaking her finger in his face. "Never assume that you're even *somewhat* more attractive than the Nightingale sisters. Got that?"

"Got it," Mike said, laughing as he closed the door and started over toward the rancher's truck.

Beth hugged her sister. "I love you, Alana."

"And I love you, too." She pulled back and gazed at Beth. "But you do happen to look like crap right now."

"So do you."

"But Mike looks worse, right?"

Beth grinned. "Right. Always worse than us. Because we are the one, the only—"

"Nightingale Sisters!" they shouted together.

ALANA AND MIKE remained in a cheerful mood all the way back to the hospital, but the closer they got to town, the quieter Beth became. She tried to tell herself everything was fine, but she didn't believe it.

Mike even resorted to some gentle teasing as they left the truck and started toward the hospital entrance. "Hey, Gloomy Gus. News flash, the good guys won."

She managed a smile. "I guess I'm a little tired."

"I think we're all running on fumes," Alana said. "We'd better stoke up on caffeine before we head back to Bisbee."

"And we're going to a coffee shop," Mike said. "I've had enough of that stuff out of a vending machine to last me the rest of my life." He ushered them through the door ahead of him. "You two beautiful ladies may go first," he said.

"Now you've got the idea," Alana said. "Training, right, Beth?"

"Right."

Mike and Alana continued to joke with each other as they continued on toward Ernie's room, but Beth's stomach twisted with anxiety as they neared the nurses' station for Ernie's wing.

Judy, Ernie's favorite nurse, was there. She looked up as they approached.

When Beth saw Judy's expression, she knew. She put her hand over her mouth to hold back a sob.

Judy came toward them, looking directly at Mike. She held the jaguar tooth necklace in one hand. "I'm sorry, Mike. Your father—"

"No!" Mike roared. He pushed past her and raced down the hallway.

Beth ran after him, with Alana at her heels.

He burst into the empty room, where the bed was already stripped, then bolted out again, running straight toward Judy. "Where is he? Where have you taken him?"

Judy put her hand on his arm. "He's being kept...somewhere else. We tried to reach you, but we weren't sure if you'd be back tonight, so—"

"What do you mean, *being kept* somewhere?" Mike stared at her, obviously refusing to hear the truth.

Alana started to sob.

Beth walked over to Mike and slipped her arm around his waist, holding on tight. Fine tremors ran through his body. "We'd like to see him, Judy," she said.

"Of course. Come with me." Judy started down the hallway.

Beth tried to urge Mike to follow Judy, but he wouldn't budge. Instead he began to shake more violently. She wrapped both arms around him and held on as the trembling became sobs. At last he crushed her against him and buried his face against her neck. "Don't leave me, Beth," he cried brokenly. "Don't ever leave me."

She could barely speak, but he needed to hear her voice. "Never," she whispered fiercely. "I love you, Mike. I always have, and I always will."

BETH NIGHTINGALE officially promised to love and cherish Mike Tremayne, forsaking all others, on a warm afternoon in October. She suffered a few prewedding jitters, especially when she allowed herself to remember that her prospective groom had run out on a similar event eight years ago. But Mike showed no sign of leaving this time.

Most of the town, invited or not, came by for the ceremony. Beth chose to hold it outdoors in a ribbon-and-flower enhanced area of the quaint little park on Main Street, conveniently located just below the Copper Queen Hotel, where preparations for a wedding dinner were underway.

Alana was Beth's maid of honor, and Mike's best man was Jack Nesbitt, his best man from his first abortive marriage attempt. Jack had moved to California and was now running a flight school. Mike invited him to try the whole thing again, and this time Mike promised to go through with the ceremony. Jack flew his own plane over for the occasion.

Beth wore a wide picture hat and a flowing dress of old lace. Alana, with Beth's blessing, wore a stunning shade of royal purple. Mike surprised everyone by insisting on a tux for himself and Jack. "Because you're worth it," he'd told Beth. "And I'll bet it's been part of your fantasy all along."

The wedding fulfilled every nook and cranny of her fantasy, from the bouquets of flowers dangling artfully from the trees to the look of pride on Mike's face as he waited for her to begin walking down the makeshift aisle between rows of folding chairs. The vows were to be exchanged beneath a latticework arch that Beth and Alana had transported to the park and decorated with flowers. To one side of the arch was a wrought-iron stand displaying Beth's wedding gift to Mike, the circle of stained glass titled *The Embrace*.

Beth had chosen to walk down the aisle alone, although she'd confided to Mike and Alana that she wouldn't be alone. With each step she took, Pete would be on one side and Ernie on the other. She'd finally told Mike and Alana about her vision on the night of the storm, and the three of them had decided their fathers had joined forces one last time to pull their kids out of a jam.

The recorded music began, and Beth started walking in measured steps toward Mike and her new life. And as she'd expected, she felt the presence of Pete to her left, and Ernie to her right. By the time she took Mike's hand and faced the minister, she was battling tears of joy.

Mike squeezed her hand. "I love you," he whispered.

"I love you, too," she murmured around the lump in her throat.

The precious words were spoken, her mother's wedding ring slipped on her finger, and then, at last, Mike's strong arms held her close. "Forever," he murmured, just before he kissed her.

Alana let out a whoop, and the assembled guests followed suit.

Mike lifted his head and smiled at Beth. "We're a hit, Mrs. Tremayne."

"Ready to party, Mr. Tremayne?"

He rolled his eyes. "If we must." He started with her down the aisle amid cheers and congratulations. "But once it's in full swing, we're sneaking out," he said in an undertone.

"Whatever for?" Beth said, smiling at everyone as Mike whisked her along.

"I'm dying to find out what sort of sexy stuff you bought to go under that very proper wedding dress."

Beth thought of the risqué white satin garments that moved so deliciously against her skin as she walked. "Just the basics."

"I don't believe it."

"Goodness, what sort of woman do you think I am?"

"Just the sort I want."

And at long last, Beth knew that it was true.

WELL, PETE, WE DID IT. Wasn't easy, but danged if we didn't pull it off.

Looks like it. I've never seen Mike or Beth looking happier. Even Alana seems to be glowing today.

Probably has something to do with that Jack fellow. He's been making cow eyes at Alana, and every once in awhile I notice her lookin' back.

You know, Ernie, I can't say I'm surprised about that. I guess I never told you, but Jack got drunk at the rehearsal dinner eight years ago, took me aside and poured out his heart. Seems he'd loved Alana for years, but he hadn't said anything because she was Mike's girl, and Mike was his best friend.

So why the heck didn't he move in when Mike moved out?

He tried. She wouldn't have anything to do with him.

Looks like a different story, now. She's sittin' next to him, flirtin' to beat the band. She'll have him drinkin' champagne from her shoe before the night is over.

Speaking of that, Ernie, my friend, pass the bottle.

With pleasure. Want one of my cigars? They're imported.

You know what, old buddy? I just think I might.

BETH GLANCED AROUND at her guests as they enjoyed the wedding supper she and Mike had planned so carefully. She sniffed. Then she leaned toward Mike. "I smell cigar smoke."

"Nobody's supposed to be smoking in here." Mike took inventory of the room. "Must be coming from outside the dining room. Nobody has a cigar, Beth."

She sniffed again. "But it's so strong. And it smells like...never mind. I must be going crazy."

"No, you're not," Mike said quietly. "I smell it, now, too."

She looked into his eyes, and there was a suspicious sheen of moisture there. A lump formed in her throat. "Mike, you don't suppose...?"

His voice grew husky. "That's the brand he used to buy when there was a really special occasion. And this certainly qualifies."

"It could be somebody passing by who smokes the same brand."

"Or maybe he's here, sharing our happiness." He took her hand and laced his fingers through hers. "After all, you just agreed to be my wife. Miracles are happening all around me today."

"That's a lovely thing to say."

His grip tightened. "I have a few more up my sleeve. Come home with me and you'll find out what they are."

"Now?"

"They'll never miss us. And I want so much to be alone with you."

Beth slipped her hand in his. "Then I'm all yours."

Is it much trouble to get these cigars, Ernie?

Why, Pete?

Take a look at where the happy couple is headed.

They're sneakin' out!

They sure are. And unless I'm mistaken about how these things go, we'll need another box of cigars before you know it.

Hot diggity dog. Grandbabies.

**Don't miss the red-hot sexy reads from
Temptation's® BLAZE**

Turn the page for a sneak preview of

Scandalized!

by
Lori Foster

Scandalized!

Lori Foster

Out of sheer necessity, he pulled the car off the main street and onto a small dirt road that led to a dead end. When Tony was younger, he and his brother had come here to make out with girls. In those days there was a wide cornfield, but it had been replaced by a small park with a street lamp. Obviously things had changed, but the premise was the same. Isolation.

Despite the fact that he was sweating, he left the car running, for it was a cold night in early November. He killed the lights, though, giving himself some illusionary concealment. When he turned to face her, he already had his mouth open to start his argument, but he was brought up short by the picture she presented.

Moonlight poured over her, revealing the sheen of

dark hair, the shape of her ears, her high arched brows.
Her eyelashes left long feathery shadows on her cheeks
and shielded her eyes from his gaze. Her hands were
folded in her lap. She appeared somehow very unsure
of herself...vulnerable. It wasn't a look he was used to,
not from her. She lifted her gaze to his face, and once
again he felt that deep frustration.

It wasn't that Olivia was beautiful. She was by far
the most elegant woman he'd ever known, but she
wasn't classically beautiful. He had dated more attractive women, made love to them, had long-standing af-
fairs with them that had left him numb. But Olivia was
the only woman whose personality, intelligence and
disposition were attractive enough to entice him into
asking her to carry his child. That was something.
More than something, actually, when you figured it
was usually looks that drew a man first, and the other,
more important features of a woman that kept him
drawn.

When he remained quiet, she said, "I know what I'm
asking seems absurd. After all, you could have any
woman you want, and after knowing you for so long,
it's obvious you don't particularly want me. That's
okay, because up until you mentioned your plan, I
hadn't really thought about wanting you, either.

"But you see, I've made my career everything." Her
hands twisted in her lap and her voice shook. "Just as
you don't want any involvements now, neither do I.
That's why the idea seems so perfect. I haven't taken
the time or the effort to get to know very many men,

and almost never on an intimate level. These days, only an idiot would indulge in casual sex. But starting a relationship isn't something I want, either. So I thought, maybe we could both get what we wanted."

Tony searched her face, feeling dumbfounded. Surely she wasn't suggesting what he thought she was. "I want a baby. What is it you want, Olivia?"

She turned her head away from him and looked out the window. Sounding so unlike herself, she whispered in a small voice, "I want a wild, hot, never-to-be-forgotten affair. For two weeks. If during that time I conceive, the baby will become yours, and we'll go on with the rest of your plans. If I don't conceive, I'll be on my way and you can find another woman who, hopefully, will prove more fertile. You won't owe me a thing.

* * *

Temptation® turns up the heat in BLAZE.
Look out for Scandalized! *by Lori Foster,*
available this month in Temptation®.

Spoil yourself next month
with these four novels from

HOLD THAT GROOM! by Leandra Logan

Grooms on the Run

Bridal consultant Ellen Carroll had created the perfect wedding
for her best friend. But the bride had forgotten one small detail—
to ask the groom! Harry Masters was shocked and Ellen couldn't
blame him. Especially when she realised Harry was totally
wrong for her friend but totally right for her!

COURTING TROUBLE by Judith Arnold

Sophie Wallace and Gary Brett had better things to do than jury
duty. However, once they met each other in the courtroom, things
began to look up. Trouble was they were working on a case about
a bride suing her groom for jilting her. While Sophie had every
sympathy for the bride, Gary was siding with the groom!

HEART AND SOUL by Susan Worth

It Happened One Night

Kat Kylie and J.P. Harrington were both risk takers. But this time
Kat had lost a gamble and feared she stood to lose her
independence, too. After one night of steamy sex—she was
going to have a child who would rely on her. And a man who
would go to the ends of the earth to win her...

A HARD-HEARTED HERO by Pamela Burford

Tough ex-commando, Caleb Trent feared he was losing his edge
living in such close proximity with Elizabeth Lancaster. He'd
had no problem 'kidnapping' her out of a risky situation. But
keeping her captive was hard on his ego—and his libido.

On sale from 10th August 1998

MILLS & BOON®

Penny Jordan

COLLECTOR'S EDITION

Mills & Boon® are proud to bring back a collection of best-selling titles from Penny Jordan—one of the world's best-loved romance authors.

Each book is presented in beautifully matching volumes, with specially commissioned illustrations and presented as one precious collection.

Two titles every month at £3.10 each.

4 FREE
books and a surprise gift!

We would like to take this opportunity to thank you for reading this Mills & Boon® book by offering you the chance to take FOUR more specially selected titles from the Temptation® series absolutely FREE! We're also making this offer to introduce you to the benefits of the Reader Service™—

★ FREE home delivery
★ FREE gifts and competitions
★ FREE monthly newsletter
★ Books available before they're in the shops
★ Exclusive Reader Service discounts

Accepting these FREE books and gift places you under no obligation to buy, you may cancel at any time, even after receiving your free shipment. Simply complete your details below and return the entire page to the address below. *You don't even need a stamp!*

YES! Please send me 4 free Temptation books and a surprise gift. I understand that unless you hear from me, I will receive 4 superb new titles every month for just £2.30 each, postage and packing free. I am under no obligation to purchase any books and may cancel my subscription at any time. The free books and gift will be mine to keep in any case.

T8YE

Ms/Mrs/Miss/Mr.....................................Initials ....
BLOCK CAPITALS PLEASE

Surname ....

Address ....

....

....Postcode.............................

Send this whole page to:
THE READER SERVICE, FREEPOST, CROYDON, CR9 3WZ
(Eire readers please send coupon to: P.O. BOX 4546, DUBLIN 24.)

Temptation is a registered trademark used under license.

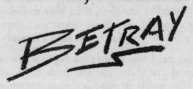